D1798475

Letchworth Writers

2018 ANTHOLOGY

Compiled and Edited by
Paul Walker & Len Maynard

Letchworth Writers

We are an informal gathering of enthusiastic and supportive writers, who meet regularly to exchange critiques, undertake creative writing tasks and talk about ways to improve our craft. The stories in this anthology were written by group members.

Letchworth Writers' Group is a part of Letchworth Arts and Leisure Group
www.lalg.org.uk/writersgroup

Contributors:
Len Maynard
Hrubadour Tusk
Sheila Molloy
Alan Davie
Caroline Markovitch
David Strong
Diana Newson
Charlotte McDermott
Paul Walker
Emma Branch
Chris Rawlins
Marjorie Allwood
Erol Hasan
Rose Saliba
Virginie Busette
Imelda Harrison

First published in paperback by Letchworth Writers in 2018

CONTENTS

I'm Here (A Christmas Ghost Story), Len Maynard 5
Islanders, Hroubadour Tusk 26
Day Zero! Sheila Molloy 31
Bella, Alan Davie 36
The Samphire Box, Caroline Markovitch 42
Barry, David Strong 47
A Thirsting, Len Maynard 55
Playing down at the brook, Diana Newson 58
Blue Waters, Charlotte McDermott 59
Details, Charlotte McDermott 62
Violin Lessons, Paul Walker 68
The Voyage, Emma Branch 76
The Money Tree, Sheila Molloy 82
Treasured Island, Chris Rawlins 86
Images, Len Maynard 90
My Station in Life, Diana Newson 111
The Sound of Silence, Emma Branch 119
A Kitten Christmas, Marjorie Allwood 123
My sister's child, Diana Newson 129
Out of the Earth, David Strong 130
Rebirth, Erol Hasan 141
A Monstrous Mother Murderer, Sheila Molloy 147
The Prince-Frog, Hroubadour Tusk 156
I Was Not Happy, Alan Davie 162
A Shared Secret, Paul Walker 168
Flour White and Spindle Thin, Len Maynard 173
Cash Cow, Hroubadour Tusk 203
Frank, Paul Walker 208
Lights, Chris Rawlins 212

Lord and Lady Moneytree, Charlotte McDermott	214
Summer, David Strong	218
Life Lines, Caroline Markovitch	223
Kismet, Emma Branch	228
Ding Dong on High, Chris Rawlins	232
Auxilium Sui, Alan Davie	235
Disappear, Charlotte McDermott	241
Trees, Diana Newson	244
Journey to Soweto, Rose Saliba	245
Door, Paul Walker	249
Food, Diana Newson	253
Boy in a Suitcase, Virginie Busette	258
A Lucky Break, Sheila Molloy	260
Lost and Found, Charlotte McDermott	264
Switch, Virginie Busette	267
Lucky Lucy Valentine, Imelda Harrison	271

I'm Here

A Christmas Ghost Story

Len Maynard

It didn't feel like Christmas morning.

It was unseasonably warm, but a steady drizzle fell from a leaden sky, dampening his spirits even further than they had been when he'd surfaced from a restless sleep a little before dawn.

William Burton switched on the wireless and made a pot of tea while he waited for the valves to warm up. As the melodic voices of the Westminster Abbey choir filled his tiny kitchen with a rousing carol, he stared at the gilt-edged invitation leaning up against the milk bottle on the kitchen table, and shuddered. The invitation to the Mayfield's Christmas party had dropped through his letterbox onto the doormat two days ago and had rested there, against the bottle, ever since.

As the choir launched into a robust rendition of *Oh Come All Ye Faithful*, Burton snapped off the wireless and went to the bathroom to shave and get himself ready.

The drive up to Suffolk, and the Mayfield's house, which was situated in a small village just outside Bury St Edmunds, was easy. There wasn't much traffic on the roads at this time of the morning on this special day, when most people were sitting in their cosy homes with their families, tearing the gaudy paper from carefully wrapped presents to reveal the prizes within. The journey took him just over two hours.

The last section of the drive was through a series of country lanes, bordered by high hedges that formed the perimeters of bare, harvested wheat and corn fields, and meadowlands populated by Friesian cows and small collections of miserable, scrubby horses, their winter blankets saturated by the steady rain that fell from the sky.

He gave a sigh of relief when he finally pulled in through the gates of the Mayfield's grand country pile and pulled up next to the dozen or so cars that were already there, parked in regimented order on the wide gravel forecourt at the front of the property. These were the guests who had been invited to travel down the previous evening and who were probably now lounging around in one of the many downstairs rooms, replete after one of the Mayfield's delicious fried breakfasts.

Taking the small, gift-wrapped present from the back seat of the car he got out of his second-hand Morris Oxford and went up to the front door. As he pressed the ceramic bell-push he stared at the small parcel in his hands – a silver-plated toast rack, bought hurriedly from *Gamages* in town the day before, and wrapped, almost as an afterthought, upon rising this morning.

It was a meagre present, and would pale into insignificance next to the lavish offerings brought by some of the other guests, but it was a gesture, nothing more. He'd had to bring something with him, and he knew it would be graciously received, especially by Estelle Mayfield, who didn't have it in her heart to be anything other than courteous, but he knew equally that he would be judged by some of the others there by that gift. It would stand as a token, a symbol of his reduced circumstances and his persistent impecunity.

After a few moments the door was opened by Estelle, looking radiant in a floor-length gown of cream satin, her silver blonde hair Marcel-waved to perfection.

"William," she said. "So lovely of you to come. Welcome to Christmas 1933 at the Mayfields." She leaned forward and kissed his cheek and his nostrils were filled with the delicious aroma of *Chanel No.5*, a fragrance he knew so well, and always associated with her. "We're in the morning room. Come through."

Burton followed her into the house. The huge hallway had almost been taken over by a massive Christmas tree whose branches reached up to within a foot of the ceiling. Richly decorated in red and gold baubles, with a smattering of tartan, a nod to Mayfield's supposed Scottish heritage, the tree spoke of opulence and wealth befitting a family of the Mayfield's social standing, but Burton remembered times when Laurence Mayfield's wealth had been far less than his own, the times when Estelle was his own true love, his intended, his wife to be. But that was before the Great Depression.

In 1930 Burton had seen his fortune vanish within the space of a year. Poor investments, and reckless spending on a number of business ventures that turned into white elephants, had seen his wealth wither to its current parlous state.

While William Burton's fortune dwindled, so Laurence Mayfield's increased. Never one to take his own financial advice, despite giving it wholeheartedly to others, Burton included, Laurence Mayfield rode out the economic storm, and watched his fortune grow.

"Look, everyone," Estelle announced to the room, "William Burton's here."

A half-hearted cheer rippled from the assembled guests and Mayfield was on his feet, striding across the room to shake Burton's hand warmly.

"Good to see you, Bill. An easy drive I take it."

"Not too bad at all," Burton said. "I came up on the back roads. Not a lot of traffic really."

"A shrewd move," Mayfield said. "Frank Parsons came up last night and was stuck on the Great Cambridge Road for over an hour. That's right, Frank, isn't it?"

Parsons, an elderly bank-manger type with a paunch and a shrivelled wife, gave a nod and a grimace.

"We'll be eating soon," Estelle said. "I hope you're hungry, William, we have a five-bird roast, and our new cook's made a plum duff for dessert, as well as her special Christmas pudding. She made it over two months ago and has been drizzling with brandy nearly every day – she's so clever – a real find."

'Lovely, I'm sure" Burton said and handed her the present.

"Oh, William, you shouldn't have," she said. "I'll put it under the tree for later."

Mayfield slapped him on the back. "Thank you, Bill, but you *really* shouldn't have bothered. I know things are tight with you at the moment."

"I can afford it," Burton snapped at him.

"Hey," Mayfield said. "Easy boy. Don't take offence."

Estelle was looking at him, a sad expression in her eyes. "Larry didn't mean anything by it, William, I'm sure."

Burton shook his head. "Sorry," he said. "I'm a little strung out... after the drive, you know?"

"Of course," Estelle said kindly. "Go and join the others. Sit yourself down and Larry will get you a drink." She wafted out of the room and Burton made himself comfortable on one of the three large leather Chesterfields.

* * *

Dinner was served in the Mayfield's spacious and rather lavish dining room. A huge mahogany table dominated the room and stood there, groaning under the weight of enough food to feed a small country.

The table seated twenty-eight and every seat was taken. Mayfield sat at the head in an antique oak carver whilst Estelle sat to his left on one of the leather-upholstered chairs that matched the mahogany of the table.

Burton sat halfway along on the right-hand side, between Parsons, who was indeed a banker, and a man who introduced himself to him as Wilfred Cooper, an architect who lived in Hertfordshire. From where he sat, he could see Mayfield and Estelle, and he could feel only envy watching the way they hung on each other's every sentence, and laughed enthusiastically at the weak Christmas cracker jokes and riddles.

Reluctantly he accepted the offer of a party hat from Agnes Parsons who was sitting opposite him and who had pulled a cracker with him, and had insisted he place the cerise paper crown on his head. He looked ridiculous and was starting to wonder why he had come, when all his instincts had warned him not to.

"We'll listen to the King on the radio and then we'll play some games," Estelle announced as a whole Stilton was brought to the table, and the guests who hadn't gorged themselves on the roast dinner, duff and pudding, started to make inroads into the blue-veined cheese wheel.

As port was served and cigars lit, the wireless was switched on and hummed into life. An air of expectant excitement settled over the room, and then a radio announcer made the introduction.

"This is the BBC's Empire Service. And now a Christmas message to you all from our sovereign, King George the fifth."

A hush fell over the dining room and the King's voice intoned from the radio's large speaker.

The royal message washed over Burton. He wasn't listening. There was nothing the monarch could say that would make him feel better about his own disaster of a life. Instead he stared at his old friend Mayfield, puffing away on a fat Havana cigar and sipping at a ruby red glass of fine port, at the same time as using his knife to pop crumbs of Stilton into his mouth.

Burton glanced up at the long case clock that stood against the wall and watched as the minute hand crawled slowly around the etched and engraved silver dial. He was counting the hours before he could respectfully leave here and make the drive home.

After what seemed a lifetime the King finally stopped droning on.

"Let's play a game." The speaker was Agnes Parsons. The dinner had certainly given her a new lease of life. It was that or it may have been the red wine she had been constantly sipping throughout the meal.

From the wireless a familiar drum roll introduced the National Anthem and the people around the table got to their feet. As the last bar of the anthem faded away they resumed their seats, except for the Mayfields. Laurence Mayfield went across to the wireless and switched it off and Estelle clapped her hands together to draw everyone's attention.

"Let's retire to the morning room. There are cards for those of you who want to play, or backgammon if you need something a little more taxing, and those of you who want to take forty winks... well, feel free. We're not going to stand on ceremony here." She turned to her husband. "Larry, perhaps you can prepare the drawing room for party games."

"But of course, Poppet," Mayfield said with a smile, and everyone trooped out of the dining room.

Burton had no interest in playing mindless card games, had little desire to play backgammon, and wasn't in the slightest bit tired. Instead he positioned an easy chair in front of the French doors, and stared out at the winter garden Mayfield and his gardening staff had created, until the light faded from the sky and the conifers and clipped topiary shapes of box and privet blended into the shadows, and it was time for the games.

* * *

"So, what are we going to play?" Laurence Mayfield said as everyone assembled in the drawing room. The centre of the floor had been cleared, all the chairs pushed back to the walls. A slightly smaller cousin of the Christmas tree in the hall stood in the corner, this one festooned with pine cones threaded onto string, tangerines that hung from silken nets, and small electric lights in gaily coloured holders shaped like fairy carriages.

Burton found himself a seat in the far corner of the room and sat there as the party guests called out their suggestions for games they could play, each one more preposterous and unappealing than the last.

"Charades!"

"Blind Man's Bluff!"

"Squeak, Piggy, Squeak!"

"Oh I know," Agnes Parsons cried. "Let's play 'I'm Here'! I love that game. Such fun."

There was murmured assent from the assembled thong.

Agnes Parsons was beginning to emerge as the life and soul of the party, Burton thought sourly. Trust her to suggest a game that he'd never heard of. It was bound to be awful

"Cheer up, William. You look like you've swallowed a cupful of vinegar with a salt chaser."

Burton jerked around and stared into the smiling face of Estelle who had taken the seat beside him. Above the smiling face the silver-blonde hair was still trapped in the elegant Marcel-waves. She was now wearing red velvet, although he had not seen her go and change. She'd applied make-up to her porcelain skin, and her cheeks glowed with the help of the artful use of rouge. Her lips were bright, bee stung, and red to match her dress, and her eyes were delicately shaded, enhancing their delicious cobalt blue and, for a moment, Burton's breath caught in his throat as the memory of losing her to the much better looking, and wealthier, Mayfield stung like a viper's bite.

"I'm not really one for games," he said, gathering himself and regaining his breath.

"Me neither," she said. "But Larry loves them, and a girl's got to do, et cetera, et cetera." She sat down next to him and took his hand. "Just watch, William. You never know, you might enjoy it," Burton stared down at Estelle's hand holding his and then looked across at Mayfield. He was watching the two of them and smiling broadly.

"Right," Mayfield said. "Who's going to go first?"

A young man with ginger, brilliantined hair, who had introduced himself to Burton as Max Shepherd, stepped forward. "May I go first?" he said.

"As if we expected anything less from you, Max?" Mayfield said. "And who wants to chance their arm against our reigning champion?"

Agnes Parsons pushed her husband to his feet. "My Frank will take him on," she said confidently.

It was obvious that Frank Parsons did not share his wife's confidence in him, but stepped forward anyway.

"He doesn't stand a snowball's chance in hell, poor devil," Estelle whispered to Burton and stood up.

Mayfield looked to her. "If you'll do the honours, Poppet."

"But of course," she said, and accepted two silk scarves from another of the guests. "If I can have the contestants in the centre of the room."

Shepherd and Parsons moved into the middle of the ornate Persian carpet and stood side by side.

Estelle moved around them until she was standing directly behind Shepherd. "If you would, Max."

Shepherd bent his knees to bring his height down to match hers. Deftly she tied the silk scarf around his eyes. "Your turn, Frank," she said, moving to a position behind Parsons

There was no need for Parsons to bend at the knee. He was slightly shorter than Estelle. He stood there with a rather anxious look on his face as Estelle blindfolded him.

"Well, spin them round," one of the guests called out.

"We'll have no cat calling," Estelle admonished the vocal guest with mock severity. "After all, we pride ourselves on being a civilized society here at Mayfields."

"Apologies, m'lady," the guest said, getting into the spirit of the proceedings.

Taking the contestants in turn by the shoulders she turned them round and around until they stood there, mildly dizzy and disorientated.

"Right, gentlemen, if you would, kneel."

Both Shepherd and Parsons did as they were told, and Estelle adjusted their positions until they were four feet apart and facing each other.

A grinning Mayfield stepped forward holding four rolled-up newspapers, bound at each end with sticky tape, and placed them on a velvet cushion Estelle now had in her hands. She walked forward and stood before Parsons. "Challenger, choose your weapon."

Tentatively Parsons obliged, taking one of the newspapers and hefting it in his hand. "*The Times?*" he said hopefully.

"Bad luck, old man, you picked the *Telegraph*," Mayfield said.

Shepherd chose next.

"Now *he's* got the *Times*," Mayfield said. "Don't worry, Frank, everyone roots for the underdog."

"Right," Estelle said. "Let battle commence and may the best man win."

A hush fell over the room, a hush broken when Shepherd called out, "I'm here!"

Parsons turned his head to the right and left, trying to ascertain the direction of Shepherd's voice, and struck out with the newspaper. His blow sailed past Shepherd's chest, the momentum of the swing sending Parsons wildly off balance, and it was only Mayfield's timely intervention that stopped him toppling to the floor.

A rather breathless Parsons thanked him and knelt up straight. He took a breath and called out weakly, "I'm here!"

Shepherd's approach was more measured. Like a big cat sensing its prey he shuffled forward a few inches on his knees, raised the newspaper above his head and brought it slashing down, catching Parsons a cracking blow across the thigh.

"No score," Mayfield cried. "Only strikes above the chest count here. Your turn, Frank."

The game continued in similar fashion and Burton watched, fascinated despite himself. As a few more blows went wide of their mark, the audience of Christmas guests joined in the battle vocally, calling their support for their favourites. One wag gave a false call of "I'm here!" and sent Parsons lurching sideways. The caller earned a reproving look from Estelle.

The result of the contest was never really in doubt. If Shepherd could not guess where Parsons was from his calls of "I'm here!" the older man's laboured, wheezing breaths were a certain giveaway.

At the five-minute mark Shepherd pulled back his arm and brought the newspaper scything down, catching Parsons on top of his bald head.

"We have a winner," Estelle announced.

With a whoop of victorious delight the young man sprung to his feet and tore off his blindfold, tossing it into the air.

As Mayfield helped a slightly dazed and confused-looking Parsons to his feet, Estelle called out, "And the next contestants, if you please." And so the ritual began again with two new guests taking their place in the centre of the rug.

The game seemed to go on forever and Burton was growing bored. There seemed to be a knockout system in play, as revellers took their place on the rug and were dispatched by their opponents.

After an hour of mindless swiping and striking Estelle raised her hand. "Time for a pause," she said. "Eggnog and cherry brandy anyone?"

With relief Burton excused himself and took himself off to one of the house's many bathrooms.

He found one on the first-floor, went inside, and locked the door. He had no real desire to urinate, but was becoming desperate for a respite from the artificial gaiety below. With a long sigh he sat down on the lavatory pan and closed his eyes.

This was his idea of hell on earth, being forced to spend his time with people he barely knew, playing puerile party games, whilst the woman he still loved with all his heart, made doe-eyes at the man who was partly responsible for his decline into penury – a man who had swooped in to take advantage of his misfortune and stolen his bride to be away from under his nose. "Merry Christmas, William Burton," he muttered to himself bitterly. "Prize fool and bloody idiot."

He came out of the bathroom after a suitable time had passed and was about to go back downstairs when he heard voices coming from along the landing.

"He's as much fun as rain in the middle of June." Mayfield's voice was coming from behind a closed door. "We should never have invited him. It was your idea, I seem to remember."

"Don't be unkind, Larry. He's on his own, living in that hovel of a flat. If I hadn't invited him he would have probably sat there with ham and eggs for his Christmas dinner, and no-one even to share that with." This from Estelle. "Inviting him here was the least I could do."

"And in trying to assuage you guilt for dumping him for someone with better prospects, who could give you the life-style you desired, you burden us all with him."

"But William's very sweet, and I did love him... once."

"But not any more," Mayfield said. "Burton is yesterday's man, and perhaps seeing us here, with all our friends, having a wonderful time, will make him realise that once and for all."

"Sometimes you can be very cruel, Larry," she said, and Burton turned on his heel and went back downstairs.

He entered the drawing room to find the party in full swing, with guests sitting, sipping from glasses of cherry brandy and eggnog, and chatting animatedly. Shepherd was holding court, regaling his fans with tales of the strategy used to defeat Parsons in the game, and another guest had started a fire in the grate of the huge baronial fireplace, and was sitting on a leather footstool in front of it, jabbing at the logs with a long, brass handled poker that had a sharp point and a wicked-looking hook at the business end for poking and turning the logs.

Burton took a cherry brandy from a silver tray on the sideboard and reclaimed his seat. A few moments later Estelle came and sat down next to him again. She stared across at Max Shepherd and clicked her tongue. "Pompous idiot," she said to Burton. "Anyone would think he had just won Wimbledon instead of knocking seven bells out of poor Frank Parsons."

"Hmm," Burton agreed. "He needs taking down a peg or two."

"Will you do it, William?"

Burton looked aghast. "Me? Good gracious, no. I've told you already, I'm not really one for games."

"Please, William," Estelle said. "I know you have the beating of him."

"Do you really think so?" Burton said, pleased, if not convinced, by her assessment of him.

"I know so," she said. "You could take on Larry next, and he'll let you win, if I ask him to. Once you've beaten him in the knockout round it will be plain sailing to reach the final to face Max."

"Why doesn't Larry take him on himself?"

"He could do, and he'd probably win, but Max works for him and it would be bad form to beat an employee, besides Larry's the host, and it would never do if he were seen to triumph in his own home." She gripped Burton's hand for the second time that evening. "No," she said. "You must do it. You have no track record in this game, and Max's defeat will be that much harder for him to bear, knowing he's been trounced by a complete novice."

"But what if I can't beat him?"

"But I have every confidence in you, William," she said. "Do it, for me, please?"

Burton demurred again, but stared at Estelle's beseeching gaze. *"Do it, for me, please."* It would be churlish to refuse, especially as the invitation to be here came from her hand. *She* had wanted him here, not her husband. He could not refuse her this one favour.

"All right, I'll do it."

Estelle's grip on his hand tightened. "Thank you so much, William," she said. "I'll go and have a word with Larry before we start again, to tell him to let you have the victory."

"Do you think he'll agree?"

"Oh, yes, he'll agree... if *I* ask him nicely."

She stood up and went off in search of her husband. Burton himself stood, and went across to the sideboard and helped himself to another cherry brandy. *Dutch courage*, he thought to himself, and smiled at the spectacle of an insufferably ebullient Max Shepherd continuing to bore the pants off his audience.

Estelle stood in the centre of the room and clapped her hands together again. "Right, everybody. Who's ready for the next round?"

The man at the fireplace stood up from the footstool. "I guess I'm up next," he said.

'I'll take you on, you old reprobate," the wag from earlier called from the back of the room.

"If you think you're up to it, Charles," fireplace man said.

"Just watch me...oh, no you won't be able to with the blindfold on. But you'll feel my victory blow soon enough," Charles the wag said.

Burton found the banter tiresome, but watched the match carefully regardless, hoping to pick up a few pointers for his own upcoming contest.

Unfortunately the match was over barely before it had begun.

Charles the wag called out, "I'm here!" and fireplace man slapped him so hard around the face with the newspaper, the wag's spectacles went flying across the room to land in the hearth next to the unburned logs. Laughter erupted in the room, led by Estelle and, for the first time that evening, Burton realised what fun this game could be.

As the laughter subsided, Estelle took her position in the middle of the room. "And our last two contestants if you please. That's you, Larry, and William, I think."

Larry strode out into the room, grinning broadly at William – why did he feel that Mayfield was mocking him? – and Burton stepped out into the centre of the rug and stood next to him.

"I'll go easy on you, old man," Mayfield said out of the corner of his mouth and gave a theatrical wink.

"Please don't pull your punches on my account," Burton said, infuriated at the man's condescension, even if it had been prompted by his beloved Estelle's intervention.

"So be it," Mayfield said. "A fight to the finish it is then."

"Yes," Burton said. "So be it."

Estelle moved behind them and Mayfield bent at the knee without being asked. Estelle tied the silk scarf tightly around his eyes. She then moved to the front and stood before Burton.

"William, hold out your arm."

Burton and did as she requested and from the sleeve of her dress she produced a red chiffon scarf and looped it around his wrist, tying the chiffon in a neat bow.

"What's this?" Burton said.

"A favour," she said.

"A favour?"

"A queen may bestow a favour to the champion of choice. This is my favour for you to wear. May it bring you good fortune. And now, the blindfold." She moved back around him and Burton bent his knees.

As she wrapped the silk around his eyes, Burton raised the chiffon scarf to his nose. The heady, intoxicating scent of Chanel filled his nostrils.

"Ready, gentlemen?"

"Of course, Poppet," Mayfield said.

"Ready," Burton said grimly.

He felt her hands on his shoulders and felt her turn him about, and then sensed rather than saw her do the same thing to her husband.

"If you could both kneel."

The hands were at his shoulders again and she was guiding him into position.

In the centre of the Persian rug Burton knelt there, his weapon gripped tightly in his fist, waiting for the signal to begin.

"William, the first strike is yours," she said, and Mayfield called out, "I'm here!"

Burton lashed out in the direction of the voice but struck only empty air. Swaying slightly, trying to recover his balance, Burton called out, "I'm here!"

He felt the breeze of Mayfield's newspaper as it passed close to his face and instinctively he swayed backwards.

"Go on Larry, hit him!" a male voice called.

"Make him pay!" another shouted.

Estelle hushed them.

Burton steadied himself.

"I'm here!" Mayfield again. The call did not come from where Burton was expecting it to be but it was too late to change direction, and again his blow sailed wide.

Damn it! He thought and adjusted his knees on the rug. "I'm here!" he called and braced himself for the impact. But it never came. Mayfield missed him again.

There were a few more attempts from either side, and perspiration was starting to dribble down Burton's back and bead on his forehead. He raised his arm to mop his brow and again caught a waft of Chanel.

There was virtual silence in the room, as if the guests were holding their collective breath. All Burton could hear was the steady ticking of the marble clock on the mantelpiece, and the occasional pop and hiss of the logs on the fire that was raising the temperature of the room, making him sweat.

And then Mayfield called again, "I'm here!" and it was as if the man was directly in front of him. Burton raised the weapon above his head, gathered himself, and brought it crashing down, relishing the soft impact it made as it collided with Mayfield's skull.

That's for losing me a fortune!

He raised his arm and struck again.

That's for mocking me!

He drew his arm back as far as it would go.

And this is for stealing Estelle away from me.

He swung his arm in an arc and made contact again, the sound of the blow making a soft, wet thwup.

Victory was his and he waited for the cheers, and waited, but the cheers didn't come. Instead the room was filled with a heavy silence.

"What's the matter with you all? I won fairly, didn't I?" Burton called.

Still the silence closed in on him. He could not even hear the clock and the crackle of the burning logs.

His fingers scrabbled at the blindfold and managed to tear it away from his eyes. As the light flooded in, he blinked several time to clear his vision.

It was then he became aware of his surroundings.

Gone was the Mayfield's sumptuous drawing room, the assembled guests and the Christmas tree with the coloured fairy carriage lights. Gone was the Persian rug. He was kneeling now on the threadbare carpet that covered the floor of his two-roomed flat in Islington.

He looked about him bleakly at the peeling wallpaper, and the chipped and cracked, yellowing paintwork. In the window was the brown and spiky skeleton of a dead Christmas tree.

As tears of realization began to dribble from his eyes and run down his cheeks, he raised his arm, to smell once more the delicious perfume suffused in the chiffon scarf tied about his wrist, and as he did so he saw the long poker with the brass handle clutched in his fist. With a cry he dropped it to the floor and saw the rusty streaks of blood staining the metal, and his eyes registered the lump of pink and bloody flesh that clung to the poker's hooked and pointed end, and the silver blonde Marcel-waved hair that grew from it.

Islanders

Hroubadour Tusk

It's always a struggle to get my flatmate Alvin to come out for a drink. Normally I don't push it – he's been through a lot. Today I had my reasons and kept persisting. He would go no further than around the corner, and only stay for a couple. To both conditions I agreed.

My route from work to the pub takes me past our flat. Alvin was waiting downstairs, looking a little agitated.

"Stressful day?" I asked. "How did negotiations with HMRC go?"

Alvin spent two and a half years stranded alone on an island. It left him with a glorious tan, but the legal authorities assumed he was dead, which meant a ton of paperwork to resolve when he was rescued six months ago.

"Yeah, stressful. I'm going in to their office to meet with someone first thing Friday. Would you be able to give me a lift on your way to work, Tusk?"

Here I interject. Tusk. That's me. I'm Tusk.

"Is that ok, Tusk?"

He was clearly apprehensive about it. Since returning, Alvin's been uncomfortable around people. He only accepted a flatmate out of financial necessity. But I think we've got a good rapport. He doesn't like asking for things, he doesn't like noise and he doesn't like being indoors. He spends his days outside in the building's courtyard, until someone comes to disturb his solitude, at which point he moves to the balcony outside our apartment.

"Absolutely Al. Yeah, I can do that. No problem."

"Thanks."

We walked down the street. I glanced over and saw Alvin was still worried about this meeting on Friday. I tried to distract him with the first question that came to mind.

"When you were on the island…"

All my questions to Alvin seem to begin that way. I don't mean to intrude upon his pain. It's just a very interesting situation, and I have a lot of questions about it. I saw him sigh slightly, but at least he wasn't obsessing over the meeting.

"When you were on the island, what did you drink? Was it water all the time? Were there coconuts? Were there enough coconuts that their milk could sustain you?"

"No coconuts Tusk. It was mostly water. I don't want to think about the times it wasn't."

My phone buzzed in my pocket as we turned the corner, facing down the pub. I checked the message. Without thinking, I spoke.

"Oh, she's there already."

Alvin stopped in his tracks.

"You didn't tell me anyone else was going to be here. I thought it was just us."

He was starting to back out. I tried to recover the situation.

"Sorry Al, I should have said earlier. But I think the two of you will really hit it off. She's very nice."

He still wasn't convinced, but if I could just take his mind off it long enough to get the two of them together. Time for another question.

"So, when you were on this island – how did it feel when you finally saw that boat coming for you? Bet you were happy to be headed home after all that time."

A response I didn't expect. A shudder before he started to talk.

"No. Not exactly."

We reached the gate. We'd made it. I opened it, and stepped into the garden, holding it for Alvin. But he hadn't finished talking.

"What you've got to understand Tusk, is... you get used to having an island all to yourself. That you can get up and walk around whenever you need. It becomes peaceful. And then, on the boat, all of a sudden you're trapped in this tiny, floating... box is what it is. And it's loud. You can hear every sound everyone makes. And all the while, all the way home, you're surrounded by people you don't know how to be around. Always knocking on the door of your cabin, always crossing your path in the corridor letting you know you're not alone anymore. Telling you with a smile that soon you'll be docking in the big city, where there's millions more people everywhere you look all the time, and you'll never really be alone again. You don't understand Tusk. It's not your fault. I don't expect you to – no one really can."

He stopped.

"I really don't think I can do this. I'm sorry. I'll see you back at the flat."

"Alvin," I had one last desperate attempt to save this. "I'm sorry. I know you're nervous. But I really want you to meet my friend. I think you might find that, actually, the two of you have a lot in common."

His eyes narrowed. He wasn't moving towards the garden, but he wasn't moving away from it either.

"How do you mean?"

"Well she had," I struggled to find the right words. I didn't want to tell her story before she did. "Sort of an unusual childhood."

A voice called out from the other end of the garden.

"Tusk!"

It was my friend. She was standing on her bench to attract my attention, long blonde hair dangerously close to dipping into her drink. The barman, collecting empties from the neighbouring tables, cleared his throat and she quickly sat back down, going red.

She had chosen Alvin's favourite table – underneath a large apple tree at the back of the garden, which covers it without cutting off the sun. A good distance from the other tables and a clear, unobstructed route to the exit. It's the table all the pigeons seem to flock to. It wouldn't be my choice, but Alvin likes it.

I turned to look at him, still standing there. He was leaning forward, curious to see who the voice was coming from. I sensed my opportunity.

"Alvin," I stepped back, letting him in. I put a hand on his shoulder and steered him towards her end of the garden before he could slip away. She stood, wiping her hands on her jeans.

"This is my friend, Rapunzel."

Day Zero!

Sheila Molloy

The red digital display read 3.30am. Phil Everdene groaned and gave up trying to sleep. Simulating energy he did not feel, he got up, put the kettle on and tried to switch off his worries by completing a Level 9 sudoku slumped on the settee. When this didn't work he booted up the computer and reluctantly addressed what really bothered him. If the payment from the customer they had chased for three months had not reached the company bank account after his plea to them that afternoon, Phil had no idea how he would pay everyone's wages or how his firm could carry on trading.

He took a sip of tea, turned back to the screen and saw some huge pulsing red letters. They read: 'Day Zero!'

'I'll be damned,' he muttered. He had forgotten all about his macabre prediction. Suddenly whether his firm was going to survive or not became irrelevant. The question now was whether he would survive the day of his own predicted death.

He made the life expectancy calculation after his elder brother Joe died of pancreatic cancer, the same disease that killed his dad. Grieving and deeply depressed, Phil had undertaken genetic counselling to see if he had inherited the same faulty gene but his scientific mind was not satisfied with the 'probably not' result. He needed more than that. Priding himself on his maths and ability to view his own mortality dispassionately, he ploughed through data used by insurance companies and the office of national statistics to create his own formula for assessing how long he would live. He was ruthlessly thorough. Not only did he factor in the family's cancer link but his GP visits and how often he had been prescribed antibiotics and other medicines. He recorded his weight, height and BMI, exercise and activity levels and alcohol consumption. He even factored in his coffee dependence and the fact that intermittent periods of insomnia made him prone to clumsiness and sloppy thinking next day.

The result was 4,055 days of life left – just over 11 years. For a time Phil had the number counting down on the top right hand corner of his computer screen. He hoped it might focus his mind on living each day as fully as possible and propel him to achieve his full potential before his time was up. However when Sonia, his wife at the time, told him he was sick to be so obsessed with his own mortality, a view reinforced by all their friends, Phil took the number off the screen. Yet he could not bring himself to obliterate it, so he secretly consigned it to a file which would be activated only on his death day when Day Zero! would flash up in big red letters.

And now that day had come. But could he trust the mathematics of 11 years ago? Was this really the day he checked out? Phil chewed a piece of skin at the side of the nail on his index finger. There were three ways to play this. Ignore it, use the next 24 hours to cram in as many pleasures as possible, or play it safe to minimise any risks he may have overlooked. The long-buried hedonist in him thought about making the day a feast of the senses. He regretted not having more warning because his long-cherished dream of paragliding over the Grand Canyon would not be feasible in the time available. But he could call up Mandy for a morning of sex and he could lunch at his favourite restaurant and order the sort of wine that had dust on the bottle. He would, of course, proposition the married waitress with gorgeous legs who had flirted with him for the past six months and have it off with her in the cupboard where they kept the table cloths. He hadn't smoked for years but he would enjoy every cancerous puff of a post-coital cigarette. He would hire a limo and chauffeur to whisk him to the Cheltenham races and bet an indecent amount of dosh on a horse, merely because he liked its name. After that would come an evening at his club gorging on high-calorie food oozing with forbidden fats. Then he would then ring a number he had not used in years, but knew by heart and get oral sex from an expert.

Phil sighed. Who was he kidding? 'Day Zero' was still flashing on the screen so he deleted it. Nonsense. Of course it was. But he phoned his PA and told her to cancel the day's appointments because he would be working from home. No reason to go out and tempt fate, even if it was rubbish.

However, because of all the tea he'd drunk during the night, Phil found himself out of milk when it came to his habitual 11am coffee fix. Still, the corner shop was only 200 metres away – not exactly a risk factor ...

* * *

Bill Riordan playfully smacked his wife Doreen on her ample bottom, then folded his arms round her waist as she stood at the sink in her dressing gown. She smelt deliciously of bed and he was tempted to ask for seconds. 'Have I told you I love you today?' he said nuzzling her neck.

'You've shown me. Now get away with you, you old fool,' said Doreen. 'Your sandwiches are on the side. Roast beef with a bit of horseradish to liven them up.'

'Wish I could stay home and just cuddle up,' said Bill. 'Don't feel that bright.'

Doreen turned abruptly, eyes searching his face. 'What's wrong?' she said.

Bill felt her stiffen and stroked her plump cheek. 'Nothing to worry about, love. Just feel a bit knackered, that's all. Old age I expect.'

She touched his forehead. 'You're sweating – hope you're not going down with anything.'

'Just getting hot and bothered being near you,' he said kissing her on the nose. He took his sandwiches from the work surface, walked into the hall and reached for his coat as pain gripped his chest.

Doreen had followed him into the hall. 'Bit of indigestion again,' he said taking a pill from his coat pocket. Nothing to worry about.'

'Got a lot of driving to do today?' she asked.

'No, just local stuff. Deliveries to a few corner shops. No sleeping in the cab tonight, thank God. Won't be late home.'

'Mind how you go then.'

At 11.10am Bill Riordan's chest clenched in agony when the massive heart attack ended his life. Phil Everdene crossing the road in front of his lorry had no time to register satisfaction that his mathematical calculations had proved correct.

Bella

Alan Davie

Bella had always loved music. At a very early age she was able to pick out a tune on a plastic keyboard or xylophone.

For her seventh birthday, after much pleading, her parents bought her a basic electronic keyboard, and within a couple of weeks she was able to play most of the pop songs she heard on the radio. Her parents should have realised that their daughter was a genius, but they had their problems and didn't notice what Bella was doing. Her Mum was going to have a baby, but it (Bella thought it would be a baby brother) never arrived and after that, her Mum seemed very sad and sat at home all day drinking, what she called, her medicine. Bella thought that her Mum didn't love her anymore and she didn't like the way her Mum behaved. Her Dad would talk to her and hug her but he wasn't around much. Most nights she heard her Mum and Dad shouting after she had gone to bed. Her Dad had something to do with building things, which meant that they travelled around a lot. Bella was never in one school for more than a few months, so she didn't have any close friends.

When Bella was twelve her Dad bought her a second-hand guitar and a book with diagrams of all the guitar chords. As usual it was not long before she was strumming like a professional. She could mimic all the current hits and even had a go at writing some songs herself. It was about this time that her Dad changed his job and was able to spend more time at home and they no longer had to move. Mum still wasn't right but she was much better than she had been.

By the time Bella was fourteen she had been at the same school for two years. After so many years of being friendless she still found it hard to make friends, but she did get on with some of the girls in the music classes; others ignored her. There was one group of older girls, who sneered at the way she dressed and called her *Frump*. These girls thought they were brilliant because they had formed a girl band called the *Fox Kittens*. They had performed at some of the school functions and had also done some gigs outside of school, friend's weddings, parent's parties, kid's discos; that sort of thing. They were quite popular locally and were so convinced that they were good they acquired a *manager* – a smarmy chancer, who told them he could get them to the top and make them famous. Admittedly, he did get them some work in local pubs and a small festival. But they didn't make any money and the manager spent most of his time patting the girls' bottoms. Bella thought the *Fox Kittens* were pretty ordinary, lacking flair, and talent.

One day Bella was amazed to hear that the *Fox Kittens'* manager had actually got them a real gig, as one of the back-up bands for *Southern Lightning*, who were to play at the local college's End of Term Ball. *Southern Lightning* was an up and coming band who had an album in the charts and a single at number seven. Their lead singer and guitarist was Jason Argon, the heart-throb of most teenage girls. Bella liked him because she recognised that he was a real musician. She would really like to get into the Ball to hear him play, but knew it would be impossible.

A few days before the big night tragedy struck the *Fox Kittens*. Courtney, their base guitarist, tripped up a kerb and broke her wrist. She turned up to rehearsal with a plaster on her arm and was devastated to find that there was no way she could play. This was their big break and it seemed to be slipping through their fingers. The girls panicked and started bickering. The manager phoned his limited contacts without success. The only bass guitarist he knew of was a fella called Rodney, but he was playing at a festival in Holland. The girls spent half an hour screaming at each other and blaming poor Courtney for their complete downfall. Courtney was in tears and about to leave when she suddenly shouted, 'What about the Frump from school? I've seen her play the guitar and the cello so she could probably play the bass.'

'No way,' was the girls' reaction. 'Have you seen the way she dresses? She would ruin our image.'

The manager said, 'I don't think we have an option. If Courtney thinks she is a possible, we have to give it a try.'

After more grumbling the girls reluctantly agreed.

'What's her number?'

'I don't know. I don't even know her name.'

'Where does she live?'

Blank faces.

'We will have to go down to the school and get her details from the office.'

They all bundled into the manager's car. Courtney stayed behind as she was in pain.

At the school they found they were in luck. Bella was in the music room practicing a cello piece for the school orchestra. They explained the situation and implored Bella to come to the rehearsal room and try the bass guitar. Bella resisted for show, but inwardly she was thinking 'Yes! My chance to see Jason Argon.'

Again they squeezed into the car, which gave the manager more opportunity to touch the girls' legs. Back at the rehearsal hall, Courtney showed Bella the pedals and amplifier controls. Bella tested the guitar with a few chords. The *Fox Kittens* were not impressed. After a little more strumming Bella remembered a bass guitar riff she had heard on a heavy metal album. She played. The sound reverberated round the room and when she finished the *Fox Kittens* and their 'manager' just sat in stunned silence.

'You've got the job. Can you make 6:30 on Saturday at the College?'

'I'll check my diary,' said Bella - joking.

The rest of the evening was taken up with rehearsing the set that they would play on Saturday. They gave Bella the chord sequences, but they were so obvious she soon abandoned them.

In a couple of the songs she was given the opportunity to improvise a solo, which she did, to applause from Courtney.

Saturday went without a hitch. Following an indifferent boy band, the *Fox Kittens* received enthusiastic applause. Then the magic began. *Southern Lightning* lit up the stage, wowed the audience and finished with three encores. Jason was incredible, the complete showman and the object of most women's desires. After the show, the organisers, the College bosses and the support bands were invited to join *Southern Lightning* for refreshments.

Everyone gathered around Jason Argon, who was charming, signed autographs and submitted to selfies. Bella was happy just to be with so many musicians. She was absolutely amazed when Jason walked up to her and said, 'Hallo, What's your name?'

'Bella' she said, and almost added 'Sir.'

'I loved your solo in that second number. I particularly liked the way you bent those minor chords.'

'Thank you,' she said again almost adding, 'Sir.' She was amazed at his recall and musical knowledge.

'How long have you been playing bass?'

'Three days.'

'I'm sorry – how long?'

'Three days – I was standing in for their injured bass guitar player. I usually play cello, acoustic guitar or keyboard, and I have tried flute, saxophone and clarinet with a little success.'

'That's amazing, I realised I was talking to a talented musician, but now I know I'm in the company of a super genius musician. How old are you?'

Bella blushed, not used to compliments.

'A gentleman never asks a lady's age'

'Whoops sorry, that puts me in my place. By the way, I like your style. That retro look is really cool. We have one more concert on this tour, it's in a town not far from here. I'd be pleased if you could come along'. He summoned his PA. 'Martin, arrange for Bella, here, to be picked up from the address she will give you and get her to Wednesday's concert and home again. Supply her with tickets and back-stage passes. How many tickets do you want?'

'Oh, just the one, thank you... No could you make it two, I'd like to have my friend Courtney with me.'

'OK that's arranged. After that we are taking a few weeks off, but in November we'll be in the studio in London. We are going to experiment with some new sounds. I'd like you to be there, I think you could contribute a lot. Martin will arrange transport, accommodation etc. Is that OK?'

'That is amazing.... I am nearly fifteen.'

'No, that is amazing. So talented and so young, the world is waiting for you. Martin will have to talk to your parents.'

Bella got home bubbling with excitement, she tried to tell her Mum and Dad what had happened but they were more interested in watching the telly. At least they weren't shouting at each other, they seemed happy. Perhaps they would be even happier when they saw their daughter on one of their TV shows.

The Samphire Box

Caroline Markovitch

The salt-worn wooden steps sag slightly as I sit. The clouds, thick and heavy with rain, billow and roll out at sea. I don't know if they are coming towards me or heading for the horizon, but there they are, just out of reach – someone else's storm.

The endless waves crackle over timeless pebbles, soothing me as I clasp my hands around a cooling mug of coffee, knees pressed together and shoulders hunched against the gathering storm.

It occurs to me that I am all I have now. No possessions, no home, no one to belong to.

Alone.

This is new to me. Until now I have always been surrounded, by people, by noise, by things.

As a child I was always collecting bits and pieces. Nothing valuable. Just things that caught my eye; beads from broken necklaces, shiny foil sweet wrappers, brass coloured coins from far-away countries and delicate shells of all shapes and hues collected from the shore next to our old beach hut.

This is where I sit now. Feeling hollow and lost.

The things I collected when I was small were kept in a small wooden crate I had found in the dunes many summers ago. It was worn and smooth, although still strong, and stamped on the side with faded lettering that read "Norfolk Samphire". For many years the box lay hidden, tucked under my bed or at the back of a cupboard. Just knowing it was there, hidden away but close at hand, gave me comfort. It was like an anchor, giving me roots, wherever I was living.

When things got too loud or too difficult I would pull the box from its resting place and sit for hours, picking through the bits and pieces I had gathered since childhood. Reassured by their familiar shapes and colours, each little object had the power to lift my spirits and keep the noise and chaos at bay.

Now, lulled by the wind and the sea, I wish I could find those things again and seek solace in their random beauty. But in my haste I left them behind.

The decision to leave was made in an instant and was all my own, but the speed of the separation left me feeling ripped from my place in time and space.

With only the clothes I stood up in, my handbag and my car keys, I walked away - from him, from the future we had planned together, from every possession. Even the old samphire box, which had been with me all these years was left, gathering dust under the bed.

My world was shattered. My husband of 6 years was not the man I thought he was. Perhaps this is something many people discover about their partners over time, but to find out in a split second somehow seems harder to grasp.

There's no denying life had been difficult for him - losing a job is never easy - but for him it cut to the heart of everything he was. Without his work he said he felt robbed of his identity and status; powerless and voiceless. But through everything I could still see the man I had first met and loved. I was sure we'd get through it together and told him his job didn't matter to me, that this would pass and we'd be stronger for it. At first he retreated into himself but then, as the months drew on, he began to struggle with his temper.

That last row began as something trivial and meaningless. An argument about a split bin bag – really, nothing important. But then he seemed to explode, like a trigger had been pulled and all his rage and anger was released at once.

It only took one blow. One violent, stomach-wrenching punch that knocked me backwards and threw my world into a spin. My ears rang as the skin flared red and blood trickled from a small split in my cheek where his wedding ring had made contact.

His remorse was instant. He cried and begged forgiveness, holding onto my sleeve as I staggered to my feet. I opened my mouth to speak, perhaps to forgive him, cradle him and let the incident drift unspoken into the pages of our past, but when no words come out the moment was gone. There could be no forgiveness. This was unforgiveable.

By now he was on the floor, half kneeling, crouched and crying. I stepped over him, picked up my brown leather bag and walked out of the front door, propelled by shock.

I came to the only place I could think of; the beach hut my parents had brought when I was a child. A place of safety and calm that was left to my sister and me when they died. I suppose the idea was that we would visit and relive the memories of long hot summers by the sea, but despite good intentions this never really happened, and the beach hut had been left to splinter and fade against the shingle shore.

Now, as I pick at the traces of lemon-yellow paint still holding fast to the knots and whorls of wood I can still feel the ghosts of our childhood laughter. But even surrounded by warm memories of a safe and happy family I am still brittle and fragile.

Of all the many losses I have felt since closing that front door, the one that resonates most deeply is the loss of my treasures in the old samphire box. Without these things to ground me I feel adrift and alone in an unpredictable world.

I let the cup fall from my hands and clench my fists, partly in anger, partly in despair. What will I do now?

The breeze that whips at my hair is edged with a chill, but in its breath I think I hear a whisper of hope.

"Begin again."

Maybe the voice is in my own head, but the message is clear. I uncurl my legs from under me, sitting a little straighter. I will not let this sink me.

At my feet I notice a small spiral shell; dull, white and rough on the outside with specks of mother of pearl catching the weak winter sunlight. I pick it up and turn it over in my hand, letting my fingers trace the sea-tumbled edges. Then, almost as a reflex, I slip it into my pocket.

With the shell safely stowed, I lift my gaze to the fat, grey storm clouds now drifting away from my place on the shore and off out to sea. I understand in that instant that I will heal. I will use all my strength and resilience to find myself new roots. This is my new beginning.

Barry

David Strong

His name was Barry. And like a lot of intelligent animals he recognised his name when called; and if he felt like it, or could be bothered, he would come over and say hello. But what made Barry different was that he could say his own name. Oh; it was only a smack of the full lips and a guttural grunt – but, Barry was an intelligent ape, he knew it was his name.

And that kind of awareness made him extraordinary.

Barry had a personality. He was so laid-back and casual, after all, he wanted for nothing; he had a mate, he had constant easy food and space to move around, swing, exercise, play, scratch, yawn... and he would spend days just watching the world go by. He was special. It started off as a study into Alzheimer's and other neurodegenerative disorders. His ancestors had had their gene sequence manipulated and he had had various tiny neural prosthetic devices fitted when he was very young.

Because of his genetic and anatomic similarity with humans, Barry had been involved in drug trials which had proved of enormous help in the understanding and reactive consequences of stimulants and preventatives. He had taken it all in his stride with a pleasing attitude and a reassuring dependence on his human friends even when the trials had left him temporarily debilitated and ill. Barry was regarded as an outstanding and successful study.

But over the years it had had its effect on him, he was moody, often grumpy and quiet, but then he would soon return to his jovial, calm and pleasant ape-ness. There had as well, been outstanding improvements in his levels of forced intelligence, in his self-awareness, and his motor skills and his special awareness.

With a vocabulary of some 1000 words in sign language and recognition he could understand concepts like pain, cleverness, fear, happiness, humour. There was an undisputed level of hominid sapience not seen before...

* * *

Barry had years of tests which he had undergone with a resigned acceptance and aptitude which had pleased, surprised and then astounded the people who worked with him. To begin with he was keen and eager to please, he really seemed to enjoy the tasks given to him, seemed to relish and appreciate each morsel of prize and attention.

He would accomplish quite complicated logic problems and was rated at his best with an IQ of 72; he could add up and subtract simple numbers; he could visualise and pretend; play and laugh, to see him laugh was a joy. But all these tests were nothing. They proved little. Barry was a new species. He was a manipulated hybrid, he was a changed creature who could talk to those that studied him. That was the magic of Barry. Conversations were basic. But you could talk in sign language, in grunts and touches, points and gesticulations.

'Hello Barry'

'B – rry hap-pee!'

<Breakfast Barry? Want fruit, nuts, juice?> signed Eibhlin.

'B-rry' < Juice.> and he signed with his right hand and fingers for his favourite juice. He pointed to his bedding corner and made a sign by pinching his squat, flat nose with his thumb and forefinger – Eibhlin laughed and made a poo-ing smelly sound. Barry laughed with her, like a chattering, slapping sound with his lips and tongue; and his eyes. Barry was a pleasure to be with when he was happy. Eibhlin roughly scratched his shoulder, he was three times her size of her small frame but she did not feel threatened by him, they were friends.

<Eibhlin change your bed – nice smell.> she signed.

He asked when he wanted the toilet, he asked and chose his food when he wanted it, he liked company – he talked about the weather, about his home. But when you looked into his eyes… then you knew the sadness that Barry had to face up to with his world. He knew he was different. He did not have the same connection with his mate Lena. They watched him as he had sex, and he knew they were watching. They watched him as he tried unsuccessfully to talk with Lena, she did not understand that he was trying to talk; and they watched as he grew irritable and impatient with her.

Barry and Lena had been together for six years, well, together was rather a loose term, they did not co-habit, but they saw each other often and spent special time grooming and enjoying each other's company. They had had a successful mating twice, the first time producing a male infant who had unfortunately died young; the second time producing a very rare in breeding in captivity set of twins. The infants were doing very well. But they did not come and visit.

* * *

And Barry, as the years went by became older. And wiser? Maybe. Certainly he was more familiar, more aware of his surroundings. The tests became fewer, they no longer tried to change him, to improve him, the drugs stopped. There was not a lot else they could learn from Barry. As a subject he had really exhausted all the possibilities and the scientists realised that they could not go much further with him, he was becoming tired easily and his attention span was not that of a younger Barry. They had decided to eventually, gradually, put him into retirement, not suddenly overnight, but he would be happier and more content going to some cosy corner of a zoo where he could live out his remaining years watching people watching him as they went past. Barry was well known, the public would love to see him, they could have special sessions where Barry could show off his prodigious and precocious talents – the public might even be happy to pay...

They became, however, more interested and impressed by Barry's offspring. Penny and George had had a hereditary gain, an unprecedented definite sign of evolution in just one generation. They had a cognitive special awareness, an ability to learn sign and a dexterity of fingers and lips that had come easily, almost naturally, that had had to be taught over years with Barry. Every test was off the scale, amazing.

They understood the counting concept very quickly, even hinting at the ability to take it a step further and be able to count in fives – hands. Two hands and two fingers making twelve; four opened and closed hands and one finger making twenty one. Their concept of pretence and humour were advanced, both together and individually. They loved playing hide and seek with toys and food and laughed as each other's climbing and acrobatic antics. A similar lip and tongue smacking and clacking laugh that Barry had.

The scientists had so much to learn from the twins. So much to teach them and then to observe. And the propensity for clinical and medical research was inexhaustible. They would prove to be special subjects – after all, they were twins – that made them the perfect couple and the comparisons between reactions to drug trials to each and both would be ideal.

The friendship between the ape siblings was astonishing. They played and fought one another in play, they groomed one another, snuggled up to each other as any other ape young. But the level of communication was unique. They were taught to sign, they were taught vocal sounds but they took this learning one step further between themselves. The scientists had them on 24-hour video and could see the private progress they were making. They were creating their own hybrid language of sound, sign and expression. Fascinating.

But they were worried about Barry. For months Barry had not been himself. He was quiet, not interested in play, off his food and... well... he looked worried. They had checked his physical health. He was fine. But he had developed a distance, a distracted look as if there was something bothering him, occupying his mind, worrying him. He would just stare into space, he would no longer look directly at people who were talking to him. He had developed a vacant look; a glance to the left or the right, as if looking as someone who was not there, it was a bit like a facial tic. And he looked disorientated, confused.

They had first noted that something was wrong some months previously, Barry used to be happy, chatty, energetic, oh, he could be a bit touchy, a bit moody, but he would always come out of it, this was different, well, he just seemed to be not himself any more. But it was the way he looked at people, his keepers his human friends that had caused them concern.

* * *

Barry's best friend was his keeper Eibhlin. She had known him since birth, sixteen years before. If anyone could find out what was wrong she could. And very slowly, cautiously, with little bits of conversation over a few days Eibhlin was worried, she thought Barry was seriously poorly... on the verge of some sort of breakdown or depression. They knew that Barry could expect to live to at least 25 years and that his physical and mental health would expect to deteriorate gradually. Perhaps all the tests, all the drugs, the operations he had undergone over the years were taking their toll and after all, he had made such wonderful progress... that perhaps they had pushed him too far. Or was it the onset of an ape version of Alzheimer's, it had been studies into the disease that had led to Barry being such a good subject. Barry was physically well, they had done bloods, urine and stool tests. His appetite was not good, but not dangerously poor and they had tried varying his diet and giving him new things to eat. But Barry was not happy.

Val was one of Barry's favourite keepers, like Eibhlin they had known each other for a long time. She had been present when his first infant had died.

<Barry want toys?>

Shake of head.

<Barry want music?>

Shake of head. Looking down at feet and picking at his toes, showing that he was not interested.

<Paddling pool and water?>

<Want to quiet and think.>

<Raining outside.>signed Val.

<Raining in my head.> signed Barry.

Barry was not as talkative as she had known him. And he was irritable, not wanting to be touched, pushing her away and barking. Then he would become quiet and reflective and start looking, staring into space as if he was trying to understand something, concentrating his gaze on something or just nothing. Eibhlin kept asking 'what wrong Barry?' but her question was ignored.

Then later that day after Barry had had his evening meal and Val had settled him down for the night he kept looking over at her, scratching his side and looking at her, deliberately concentrating on her movements.

<Barry want talk. Afraid.>

'What wrong Barry?' she asked again.

<Barry want talk. Not now. Morning. Bring Val, Eibhlin, human friends. Barry talk.>

There was a group of scientists, keepers and specialists present when Barry spoke in deliberate and careful sign language:

<You think you clever. You clever. Clever you. But you not. You cannot see it. Barry can. You cannot. You cannot see it standing behind you, watching you. It sees you and it does not like you.> The humans were stunned by his alacrity, his presence.

<And it will hurt you. Bad. Bad. But you cannot see it. Barry can... It is there now. Me afraid of it.>

A Thirsting

Len Maynard

'When was she bitten, Janine?' Donovan said.

Janine stared down at her shoes, avoiding his eyes. 'Last night. I found her in the street outside the club and managed to get her into a taxi. When we got back here, I put her to bed and she's been like this ever since.'

'You should have called me last night, as soon as it happened, not left it until this morning.'

'I didn't want to. I was frightened. I thought you'd be angry.'

'Damned right I'm angry! When she told me you two were planning a girl's night out I told her to stay away from the club. There have been four attacks that I know of in the last month. You should have kept her away from the damned place.'

Janine glared angrily at him across the darkened bedroom. 'I'm Gail's flat-mate, not her mother. As her boyfriend you know how stubborn she can be when she has an idea in her head, and I wasn't going to fall out with her over it.'

'I thought you were the sensible one,' Donovan said and crossed to the bed, gently lifting the sheet. He produced a small torch from his pocket and shone the bright LED light down at Gail's neck.

The twin puncture wounds over her carotid artery were red and angry-looking, seeping a clear fluid. Donovan let the sheet drop.

On the bed Gail stirred, her long fair hair plastered across her face with sweat. A swollen tongue flicked across her lips and her eyelids fluttered but the eyes remained shut. 'Thirsty,' she mumbled. 'So thirsty.'

Janine was at his side, her fingers gripping the sleeve of his leather jacket. 'What are we going to do, Don? She'll be awake soon.'

'I'll deal with it,' he said.

'The same way you dealt with the others?'

'Unless you have a better suggestion. Wait here and watch her while I get my bag from the car.' He peeled away from her and left the flat.

Janine sat on the edge of the bed and stroked the hair away from Gail's face. 'You'll be all right, babe,' she said soothingly. 'Jan will make it all right.' She glanced around as the door opened and Donovan re-entered the room carrying a leather holdall. He dropped the bag to the floor and crouched down to unzip it.

Janine watched as he took out a heavy rubber mallet and a two-foot length of wood, one end of which had been sharpened to a wickedly sharp point.

'And that's how you dealt with the others?' Janine said.

Donovan nodded and crossed to the bed.

'There must be a better way.'

'As I said, I'm open to suggestions.'

He positioned the pointed end of the stake above Gail's chest.

As if sensing what was about to happen Gail's eyelids fluttered again but she didn't rouse.

Donovan raised the mallet high above his head and was about to bring it crashing down when he felt a sharp pain at his throat. He managed to move his face a fraction but Janine's head was in his way as she leant over his shoulder, her sharp canine teeth buried in his neck, her mouth greedily sucking his blood, draining him of his strength and his life force.

The mallet fell from his fingers, landing on the pillow with a soft thump, an inch away from Gail's head, and the stake clattered to the floor.

Janine finally released him and let him fall. 'How's that for a better suggestion?' she said. 'I thought it was you ruining my fun, but until this morning I wasn't sure.'

On the bed, Gail finally opened her eyes.

'Are you thirsty, Hon?' Janine said, and gestured down at Donovan's still twitching body. 'Help yourself while he's still warm. There's plenty left for you.'

Playing down at the brook

Diana Newson

Over Tarzan's leap, from buttercup meadow,
to mermaid's hair hollow; listen, a merman!
Wriggle under the toppling oak
then risk the climb, to the sky, to the tree house.

Ripe acorns, and the silver moon plant,
beefsteak fungus, and deadly red weed.
Squirrels run over the sunny field corner,
I dream I could live in a tree.

I tried it on horseback later,
wanting to gallop to the dark wood edge.
We foundered at Tarzan's leap;
and I went home, boots full of water.

Blue Waters

Charlotte McDermott

I wake up and stare at the ceiling, the colour of which, forgive me, could only be described as diarrhea. My head is pounding, as if a drum kit has taken up residence just behind my eyes; one with an atrocious drummer, Ringo Star, probably. My eyes have a swimmy film in front of them and I feel bloody awful. More importantly, I can't think for the life of me where I am. I search my head for clues, like I used to when I was a young man after a splendid night on the sauce, but there is nothing...empty. Just like my homework books at that bloody school I went to. Christ on a bike, my parents must have hated me to have sent me to that place. Some bastard, what was his name? Ginger, bloody curly hair, used to piss on my bed every night, little shit. Place was full of them, only option was to become a little shit too. I'll just close my eyes for a bit.

* * *

'Mister Androo, you awake Mister Androo?'

Little Phillipino face, smiling at me as I peep out from under the covers, now she does seem familiar.

'I get you cup of tea?'

My mouth feels like it's full of jammy dodgers made of sandpaper. I try to lick my lips and start to lift my head.

'No, you stay still Mister Androo, Doctor say lots of rest.'

I look quizzical, wanting to say, Doctor?

'You had bad fall Mister Androo, bang your head.'

I take another look around me, the place starts to seem familiar, but it's like trying to recognize an old aunty at a funeral; straining to see the lady beneath the creases. I think I know this place but the word, 'Doctor' has thrown me further into befuddled, doddery old codger mode.

'Am I in hospital?'

I struggle to recognize my own voice, sounds like that of a posh old duffer, surely not me.

'No Mister Androo, you here at Blue Waters' Nursing Home. You remember me? Lei-Li? I get you cup of tea?'

I nod and smile and Lei-Li grins her big toothy grin, I think she's rather beautiful.

'Good boy, that's it. I put three sugar in for you.'

I nod, and fully, truly recognize the shit hole prison, that is now my home. The place I was sent to for bad behavior. What was my crime? I hear you ask. Old age, Sir. Old fucking, stinking, shitting, crumbling age. It's a shit sandwich, it really is. Falling over, that seems to be my new hobby, and boy do I do it well, or is it badly? Whichever way you look at it, I end up on the floor and then wake up and forget where I am.

I look up at the ceiling again, and imagine the conversation that took place.

'Shall we paint the walls a nice cheery colour?'

'No, let's paint them a lovely shade of sloppy shit, remind the old buggers what nappy wearing, shitbags they've become.'

I close my eyes again, the drumming has got louder. I'll just rest them for a bit.

'I come back later Mister Androo, with your supper.'

I smile thinking about the slop and slime she will return with, don't get me started on the filth they serve up as food in this place.

'I put telly on for you? Mister Androo.'

God no, I think, but she has already turned it on torturously loud, so I duck under my covers and wonder how much longer my sentence in HMP Blue Waters will last.

Details

Charlotte McDermott

Marge: So, shall we just go over your details Sam?

Sam: Ok.

Marge: You're 6ft and dark.

Sam: Well more like 5ft 10 and a bit greying.

Marge: Women like to hear 6 ft Sam, believe me.

Sam: Even if it's a lie?

Marge: That's an ugly word Sam, let's not use ugly words.

Sam: Sorry.

Marge: So blue eyes, I'd say lovely blue eyes and we can put GSOH.

Sam: Come again?

Marge: Good sense of humour.

Sam: Right...erm.

Marge: Now come on Sam, we all love a joke don't we?

Sam: I am not great at jokes.

Marge: Go on, I bet you are, tell me a joke.

Sam: I don't know any. Honestly I don't.

Marge: Of course you do, everyone knows a joke. Now come on Sam, tell me a bloody joke.

Sam: A bear goes into a bar.

Marge: Good, go on.

Sam: (Nervously) He says to the bartender 'Pint of beer and a packet of peanuts. And the bartender says 'Why the big pause?'

Marge: Right.

Sam: Because a bear has big paws but it sounds like pause.

Marge: I know Sam, I get it. It's very funny.

Sam: You didn't laugh.

Marge: Let's talk about hobbies.

Sam: Hobbies?

Marge: Interests.

Sam: I haven't really got any.

Marge: You must have, everyone has.

Sam: Have you?

Marge: Yes Sam, I do, lots of them, but this isn't about me, is it?

Sam: I like football.

Marge: Playing?

Sam: No, watching.

Marge: You've never played.

Sam: I was rubbish at school.

Marge: Anything else?

Sam: I can't think of anything.... I used to collect stamps.

Marge: Shall we put keen sportsman?

Sam: Ok then.

Marge: What are you looking for in a woman Sam?

Sam: I am not fussy.

Marge: Who's your ideal woman?

Sam: I don't know.

Marge: Come on man, you must fancy someone.

Sam: Can't think of anyone.

Marge: When was your last relationship Sam?

Sam: I don't have to put that, do I?

Marge: Not if you don't want to.

Sam: Good.

Marge: Was it very painful?

Sam: What?

Marge: Your last relationship.

Sam: No.

Marge: Glad to hear that. Was it you who ended it?

Sam: No.

Marge: So, she ended it?

Sam: No.

Marge: So, you're still seeing her? Really Sam, I don't think you should be here then.

Sam: There wasn't one.

Marge: Wasn't one?

Sam: There never has been.

Marge: You've never had a girlfriend?

Sam: No.

Marge: But you're 39.

Sam: I know that.

Marge: And not bad looking.

Sam: Thanks.

Marge: Well I mean, you're not dead ugly.

Sam: We'll put that shall we?

Marge: Pardon?

Sam: Quite ugly bloke, crap sense of humour and shit at sport.

Violin Lessons

Paul Walker

We were strangers, you and I.
Never met,
'til over the top through mud and wire,
we stumbled under a heavy sky
over bone cut red with iron and fire.
And there
you lay with hell etched deep upon your face,
a hand outstretched, a beseeching eye,
begging to be free from that dreadful place.
I knelt by your side.
I touched your hurt and felt your pain.
Come close, stay strong my friend, my friend.
Brother in arms, this is not the end.
I closed my eyes and said a prayer,
drew my gun and released you there.
Dearest comrade, I see you still
in laboured night and unsound day.
Your answering smile yet lingers, and found
in this scorched breast a place to stay.

Somme, Picardy, France. July 4, 1916

'Lieutenant Aldridge, thank you for being so prompt.   I understand from your mother that you're a poet as well as a musician.'

'Good afternoon, Mrs Spencer, and it's plain Mr Aldridge now. My m-mother is too extravagant in her description of my scribbles. Besides, I haven't written any p-poetry for over t-two years.'

The introductions had been completed, and for that at least, I was thankful. My stammer and trembling hands were less intrusive than I had feared. Mrs Spencer, and her daughter Matilda, were too polite to comment openly, but their eyes betrayed an understanding and sympathy that I found unsettling. I wondered how much my mother had told Mrs Spencer when she called to answer my advertisement.

It was December 1918, and the sounds and smells of the trenches were still raw and vivid. I longed for a means of escape into easy forgetfulness. Of course, I was one of the fortunate few. How many times had I been congratulated on my treaty with lady luck? I had learned that a silent smile and a dreamy stare into far space brought this unwelcome line of intercourse to the quickest and neatest ending. My mother kept a spray of lavender in my bedroom and I had also discovered that the concentration required to conjure up this heavenly smell, helped to still my unsteady limbs. As they both turned, I closed my eyes and breathed deeply through my nose.

I followed Mrs Spencer and Matilda through to a room at the back of the house. 'This is the nursery,' she announced. 'I hope it's suitable for the lessons. It hasn't been used for quite a while, and it's the furthest point from our neighbours, so the least likely for you to be overheard.'

'Thank you Mrs Spencer, this will do very n-n-nicely.'

I looked around a clean and bright room with toys neatly arranged for play. A music stand was placed in the middle of the room beside two chairs, one of which had a violin and bow resting carefully across its cushion.

I smiled at the young girl and said, 'Now, Matilda, let me hear you play a s-small piece so we can see where to start. Any piece will do.'

Mrs Spencer seemed content and left the room.

Matilda inclined her head, hesitated for few moments, then sorted through a small pile of sheet music in the corner. I settled in a chair and watched as she made her selection. She was a pretty, round-faced girl of around twelve years who had clearly outgrown the toys in the room, but kept them all ready for play, or perhaps an occasional recollection of more innocent times. She hadn't uttered a word yet, but I sensed that this was not through shyness as her bearing suggested a certain defiance. What was I about to hear? Would it be an awful screeching, or a display of glorious and youthful talent? No matter, I could bear the worst she could throw my way. I had found over the past few months that the voice of the violin had helped to dispel some of my worst memories, at least for a time. As well as taking up the bow again I had decided to place an advertisement in the local paper and offer lessons. Of course, it meant giving up my position with the shipping company and disappointing my parents, but so far I had no regrets.

The chosen piece was placed on the stand and Matilda nestled the violin under her chin. Taking a breath to compose herself, she lifted the bow gracefully, paused for a moment, then started to play. She played the intermezzo from *Cavalleria Rusticana*, and played it very well. There were a few minor technical difficulties, but it flowed with a sense of elegance and charm. She stopped playing, looked me directly in the eye, then bowed her head and rested her arms by her side. My first instinct was to applaud and congratulate her warmly, but I suspected that would be the wrong response. I settled for milder praise and, 'Good. The tone and tempo were fine, but there are a n-n-number of areas we can work on to improve.'

She inclined her head with a quizzical look. Clearly this was not the reaction that was expected.

I made a few suggestions on her bowing and asked her to repeat the few sections where her fingering lost a little control. She learnt quickly and her second full attempt was an improvement, although, for me, it could not match the magical surprise of my first hearing. We moved on to tackle a *Rondeau* by Paganini, which she had not played before. I played a few bars to introduce the piece and she listened carefully with her head tilted slightly to one side. I came to understand that this was a characteristic pose of Matilda when she considered something interesting. We continued for a while until there was a tap on the door and her mother entered the room. An hour had passed quickly, at least for me. I asked Matilda if she had enjoyed her lesson and she replied, 'I liked it well enough, thank you Mr Aldridge.' Those words were the first she had spoken during my visit.

We arranged that I would attend at 5 p.m. on Wednesdays for the next ten weeks and review progress. A longer-term commitment would depend on the review and her work at school. I came to look forward to my weekly visits. Matilda was certainly the most talented of my handful of pupils, and I believed that I had also struck up a good relationship with her, as she was responding well to my teaching. After a few weeks we began to converse more easily about the music and her technique. While she was not exactly animated in these exchanges, she showed a keen interest, talking with her head inclined to one side; an affectation which I anticipated with some fondness. We had also played a duet, which to my ears was a delight for our first unrehearsed attempt, and more importantly it was the first time I saw Matilda smile. It was also clear to me after a few weeks that the weaknesses of my body were becoming less manifest.

I was surprised when after rounding a lesson off with our second duet, she volunteered the information that, 'Father and I used to play together. He played the cello.' Later, I cursed myself for not following up this remark. Initially, it seemed like an invitation to talk further about her father, but she turned her back and busied herself with her instrument and sheet music. I detected from the slope of her shoulders that she was upset at the image she had brought to her mind, so I departed without acknowledging the bravely-spoken confidence she had shared with me.

My seventh visit was on a dark and icy January evening. The door was answered by Matilda, and although her eyes were lowered, I could see that she had been crying from the flush on her cheeks and tightly-clutched handkerchief. I followed her through to the nursery looking around for signs of Mrs Spencer, but found none. I tried to find an opening for words, but Matilda snatched up her instrument and, bypassing her usual routine of preparation, began to play. The music was restive and troubling and I was thankful when, in the middle of the piece, she suddenly stopped, bowed her head and placed her right arm over her face.

'What is d-distressing you so, Matilda?' I ventured with some misgiving.

Uncomfortable moments of silence passed, but I restrained from filling them with a repeated question or distracting remark. Eventually she turned and said, 'It's mother.' She, dropped her arms by her side, looked at me, then rested her violin and bow on a chair and explained that today was the wedding anniversary of her mother and father. Grief and pain had resurfaced at the memory of their loss and her mother had taken to her bed. She looked at me directly and asked, 'What was it like – the fighting, the killing? Was it so very horrible?'

What should I say? I wanted to put my arm around her and offer comfort, but our relationship had not yet reached that level of intimacy. I could not hide the truth and answered, 'Yes, it was dreadful.'

She nodded her understanding and this honesty seemed to provide the key for her to unlock her emotions and talk about her father. He had been a university lecturer and volunteered six months after the outbreak of the war. He had spent over a year in the south of England and was promoted to the rank of captain at the time he transferred to northern France early in 1916.

I asked when he died. 'He died in the early days of the Somme offensive, or so we were told. It was some weeks later before the news reached us. We knew there was something wrong as we had not received letters. There was an inquest. It was not clear…'

At this stage Matilda stopped to use her handkerchief and compose herself before she continued. Her mother had a visit from a soldier and a man in a dark suit and bowler. She had not been in the room, but had overheard most of their conversation outside the door. He had died from a wound that held a question. A single shot to the head from a hand gun at close quarters, and it was thought that the gun was one of ours. Her mother was questioned about the possibility of suicide and the men asked to see her father's letters. Her mother was adamant that it could not have been suicide, but the men were not convinced. Matilda thought that the uncertainty over his manner of death was the most upsetting aspect for her mother.

'I feel it too,' she said. 'It would be easier to know he had died at the hands of the enemy, however it was done, than to harbour thoughts about suicide or death at the hands of a fellow British soldier.'

With that final statement Matilda's energy was spent and she slumped into a chair holding her head in her hands.

My first thought was to excuse myself and run; to escape from Matilda and her mother and lose myself – perhaps in drink or music, or both? But there were many tens of thousands at the Somme, so the chances were small. Even so, the coincidences were telling: a soldier with the same rank; the same time; a bullet in the head from a friendly hand gun. What should I do? What would be best for Matilda and her mother? For myself? Had fortune guided me to this bond with that fateful remembrance, and for what purpose? Or was my fevered mind still so full of war that I had imagined a connection? And then I knew what I should do. I asked my *brother in arms* and the answer that returned dispelled all my uncertainty.

'Matilda, I should like to tell you a story about an incident when I encountered someone at the Somme in 1916. It's not a tale with a happy ending, but I think it may help you and your mother.'

The Voyage

Emma Branch

The Sailor

'Away boy and don't you come sneaking back,' I shouted. I could see the Captain out of the corner of my eye, so I crossed my arms over my chest and stood square across the gang plank. Edward flinched and turned looking confused and betrayed. I felt his pain like a kick to my chest. I pitied this boy, no older than my own son, whose only option was to stow away on a ship to anywhere. As the Captain turned away, I quickly felt in my pocket for a few coins. 'Here take these, lad, go quickly now, it's not safe for you here, go back home.'

* * *

The Sister

'Elisabet, wait for me,' Aleksander called as we ran up the lane towards home. I slowed until he came level. 'He's not come back yet, so that's a good sign isn't it?' I asked. Alek shrugged and kicked a stone. 'I suppose it could be or .... Yes it's a good sign,' he replied smiling unconvincingly. '10 days now, he could be in London or France or even on his way to America.'

I didn't feel so sure, but I could only hope and pray that Edward was safe. I felt responsible.

I felt perhaps he'd already thought about running away, but my saying it out loud one day whilst we sat in the boughs of the apple tree gave credence to his day dreams. I didn't want him to leave of course, I just wanted him to be safe. The Cossacks who patrolled the town took delight in beating anyone who stepped out of line. Boys his age were easy pray for a pack of grown men. I'd hidden Edward behind my skirts and smiled on more than one occasion but I couldn't be with him all the time. Mother chose to ignore my concerns, but what did she care if he came home covered in bruises. It was a simple explanation for father when he returned. She was, of course, my main concern. Her outbursts were getting increasingly violent and focused always on Edward, never the rest of us. As the eldest she blamed him for trapping her in her unhappiness. For cutting short her youth.

* * *

The Docker
I spotted the tall, blonde haired boy crouched behind some packing cases, kneeling down in the dirt of the dockside. Like a lean cat, he'd watched and waited, always alert, ducking down whenever someone moved close by. He'd stayed there watching quietly all afternoon until now it was almost dark. One of the crew who docked earlier had told us they'd found a stowaway. No surprise there really except the whole crew had taken a liking to this well-educated, nicely spoken boy. He'd

told them proudly he was Estonian, they'd laughed and ruffled his hair and agreed he was Russian now.

I would have ignored him, turned a blind eye, but Josef spotted him too. He was a huge, vicious man, always tormenting the other dockers and torturing helpless animals. I saw him sneak around behind the boy and grab him by the scruff. Josef called to me to join in his sport, but I walked away pretending not to hear. I didn't want to be party to his nasty games. The boy struggled and kicked receiving a punch to the side of the head which stilled him while Josef emptied his pockets and tipped the contents of his knapsack into the filth. Finding only a few coins he delivered a swift kick to the boy's rib cage and went in search of a public house. I left him sprawled in the mud until I was sure Josef was out of sight. 'Hey, hey boy, what are you doing here?' I asked. He looked questioningly at me as I helped him to his feet. I pointed towards the ship he'd been watching and he nodded shyly. I mimed food, bringing my hands to my mouth. He nodded eagerly so I pushed him back behind the cases and went to the shed to see what I could find. Whilst he ate I pushed a loaf wrapped in newspaper and a few bottles of beer into his knapsack, then the few Krona I had into his palm. 'Good luck boy,' I said as I turned and walked away. 'I think you'll need it.'

* * *

The Boy

I felt as though I had died and been sent to hell. Days and nights rolled undistinguished into one in the darkness of the ship's hold. The little food and drink the docker had given me was long gone and I survived by drinking water that ran down the side of the rusty hull. The ship shuddered and heaved against the waves and the wind. I prayed that I would be found, that I would be spared another day of sickness and isolation.

Memories of home filled my delirious head. Memories of father walking back along the lane in the sunset. Memories of sitting in the apple tree with Elisabet and Aleksander laughing at their mimic of the baker or our school masters. Even memories of little Oskar, learning to walk and talk, learning to climb onto mother's lap to be petted like a little lamb, learning to tell tales on me, laughing as she called me in from the garden, laughing as she beat me with the fire iron.

* * *

The Barber's Wife

Looking out of the window I called to my husband 'Otto, der schnee ist sesshaft.' [*the snow is settling*] 'Sprechen sie Englisch, Anna,' he called through from the shop, 'You must speak English if you wish to be better.' I sighed, 'Yes mein liebling.' Turning away from the steamed–up window towards the warm kitchen range I asked, 'Did you see that boy in the alley again? Shall I take him some soup?' Otto sat down at the table. 'I swear you are you determined to feed every waif and stray in London mein engel. We don't know him, we don't know where he came from. It's better that you leave him alone.'

I laughed as I ladled his soup. 'Oh that's a shame Otto. I took him some soup out earlier and he gobbled it down.' My darling husband pulled me towards him in his warm embrace. 'Really women, what will I do with you? Does he have a good coat on, it's going to freeze tonight?' 'No,' I replied, 'Just a filthy, wet sweater and he looks half starved. He told me he came off a boat from Sweden. He's a bright boy, he speaks excellent English and German. He even speaks Russian.' I sighed, looking over to the misted-up window. 'And Otto, he liked my soup, he said it reminded him of his grandmother's. I think he's a good boy Otto. He has kind eyes.' He squeezed me. 'Well, if he liked your soup I suppose you had better bring him into the kitchen then, just for tonight mind, but I swear to Gott, if he murders us in our beds, it's you I'll hold responsible.' He hugged me. 'You are too good mein engel, you are too kind.'

* * *

The Mother
'Elisabet, what do you make of this,' I demanded, waving the postcard under my daughter's nose. Elisabet took it turning it over and over in her hand. The illustration was a grainy photograph of Buckingham Palace, the back held no more than our address written in an unfamiliar hand and an English stamp. 'I can't imagine, Mother. Perhaps an absent-minded

friend of fathers.' She stretched up and placed it on the mantelpiece, smiling to herself. Men! I concluded, the stupid man was probably drunk when he posted it. I sat down wearily at the cluttered table pulling the vodka bottle towards me to fill my glass.

The Money Tree

Sheila Molloy

I ring the bell, pull back my shoulders, adopt a harmless old lady smile – benign but slightly dotty – and cradle the money tree at chest height.

The door eases open and a pale face appears. The new tenant is suspicious, a bit tentative, probably thinks I'm trying to sell her something. 'Edna, the caretaker,' I say. 'And here's a money plant to welcome you to your new flat. Let's hope it brings us all some money, eh?'

She takes it and laughs. Defences successfully breached. 'Thank you,' she says. 'Come in.' I follow her through the narrow hall to the sitting room envying her pert backside. She wears baggy grey jogging pants, and a white vest which shows off toned upper arms. Bits of streaked blonde hair have fallen out of the scrunchy high on her head. There's not an ounce of fat on this one and she glows with the sort of health bestowed by privilege.

Tiny creases appear on her smooth forehead as she looks round the room for somewhere to dump the plant she does not want. 'Bit of a mess. Not sorted out yet,' she says pulling a face at the boxes littering the room. She can't even make a decision about where to put the bloody plant. I ask you! No future captain of industry, this one.

'How about that shelf. Near your computer,' I say. 'Aren't houseplants meant to neutralise the radiation from them or something?'

'Yeah. Think I've read that somewhere, too. Why not?'

'Only if you're sure,' I say. 'It's unlucky to move a money plant.'

'No, it's fine,' she says. 'Perfect.' She plonks the plant down hard on the shelf and I wince when its leaves shudder. She offers me tea. Do I mind decaf? Is soya milk OK? I fake enthusiasm, turn my back and take a swig from the hip flask in my overall pocket while she fills the kettle. What's wrong with these young women today? Why don't they do drugs and get pissed like we did instead of obsessing about imagined food sensitivities? When did allergies become the new black? While she makes the vile-sounding and no doubt vile- tasting brew, I reposition the plant slightly and rearrange the fronds.

It's her first job after university, she tells me. Human resources. I need all of mine to listen to her drivel. Now she's started, she talks non-stop. Slim manicured fingers twirl a hank of loose hair, a habit I find particularly irritating. Daddy's put down the deposit on the flat and she's soooo excited to be in the big city. My smile has set hard as concrete but there's a twitch developing at the corner of my mouth. I fight it. It's telling me I need to yawn. I could write the script for these Home Counties types. So depressingly unoriginal. She'll use her brain for a couple of years, then put it in cold storage after being efficiently rogered by a City banker. He will dangle before her a future filled with beauty treatments and gym classes – seductive buffers against the slack skin and wrinkles of ageing. He'll throw in a nanny from a third-world country to look after the 2.4 brats who will inherit his receding chin and she will gratefully engage in the dodgy sexual practices his wife now finds distasteful. I finish the tea, leave her my phone number and tell her where my ground floor flat is in case she has problems.

Back in the chaos of my cluttered home, I take another slug of scotch to get rid of the nasty taste in my mouth, then settle back to look at the bank of TV screens, one for each of the 12 flats in the building. I tense. There's activity in Flat 6. I've been waiting for this. I flip open my notebook, pen poised, and focus. I've already identified the password but I'm not one hundred per cent sure of the penultimate letter in her memorable word. I need to be certain. Yes, this time I've got it. I take another big swig. Bingo.

I switch my focus to Flat 3. This tenant's actually done some housework. Unfortunately she's moved her money plant fractionally so the camera isn't picking up such a clear picture of the VDU. Too much of an angle. Still, she has the boyfriend over on Fridays and after a bit of fumbling on the sofa, they go to his mother's for dinner. There'll be plenty of time to do a bit of corrective housekeeping then.

I ring Hasan. 'Got some new bank account details for you,' I tell him. 'And eyes on the new tenant. Number 5's having difficulties finding the rent after our recent activity so

I'll need a plant for her replacement. Probably wise if I moved to another building soon.'

Treasured Island

Chris Rawlins

Much of the British Isles was a mess in 1946. World War II had ended the previous year with monumental damage everywhere. While England and southern Scotland had suffered the most from Nazi bombings, the Scottish Highlands were crippled in a variety of ways.

Communities in such villages as Kyleakin (the gateway to the Isle of Skye) from the mainland, had lost many of their men who had served in the armed forces. Others had been forced to operate in other parts of their country, or even England, and were reluctant to return. There were much greater opportunities elsewhere offering faster growth. One exception was Ian McCullough, a farmer's son. He had served at a naval base on the south coast of England. Ian's parents still lived in Kyleakin and he was thrilled at the prospect of returning home. When he arrived back in 1946, he was saddened by what he saw. Most of the houses were standing, but where were the villagers? Many of Ian's younger friends had been killed in action. What remained was a much older village population, with several homes left empty and in need of repair.

Ian soon decided to make Kyleakin a tourist attraction for all of Skye and to improve the local economy. His father, Bruce, was so supportive of Ian's ideas that they agreed to establish a business partnership to help Skye's tourism. They realised that the history, scenery and mountains of Skye could attract people but it needed many more visitors.

Kyleakin is the starting point for most tourists because of its close proximity to the mainland, and its regular ferry services. Once there, they would need feeding and somewhere to stay. Bruce knew a young couple, Douglas and Morag Ferguson, living outside Skye's largest town, Portree. He persuaded them to buy an old house in Kyleakin, which they converted into a four-bedroom guesthouse with a dining room. Others in the village also began to provide bed-and-breakfast accommodation under Ian and Bruce's directions, and some went even further by re-establishing a couple of village shops. The owner of the village pub was inspired to modernise and introduce an eating area, and by the summer of 1948 visitors to Skye had somewhere to sleep, eat, drink, and shop. However, those tourists without a car were often disappointed. Public transport was scarce and there was relatively little to do, except walking and climbing. Bruce and Ian had separate ideas as to how they might enhance holiday plans for tourists.

Bruce's plan was entirely accidental. He heard that a local bus company on the mainland in Mallaig was investing in a fleet of about ten new vehicles. Seizing the opportunity, he persuaded the manager to sell him one of their old buses for a very reasonable price. Bruce drove it triumphantly back to Kyleakin via the Armadale ferry. He found a young villager to drive it all over Skye, and they were in business! This allowed tourists without cars to explore Portree, Broadford, Staffin, and Dunvegan Castle. Some even went out climbing in the Cuillin Hills or just walking to admire the beautiful coastal scenery.

The service became very popular after it was advertised in the local tourist guides, and by the Scottish Tourist Board. Skye tourism began to grow steadily, helping both the local economy and the McCullough business. Ian had another idea. Fishing had always been one of his many interests, so he planned to develop fishing trips for visitors. This would enable them to take part in something more active than being driven around in a bus; and they might even return with some fish. He managed to repair an old boat which could hold up to six anglers. Some of his early trips included a number of tourists who complained that they had paid good money for a trip but had caught nothing. Since these fishing trips had all been north of Kyleakin, Ian decided to try fishing off the southern part of the island.

On one of his first trips, Ian's boat was just north of Armadale when one tourist caught a canvas bag with only a drink carton in it. Whereupon Ian gave him and the other clients a tutorial on how to catch fish such as pollock, wrasse, mackerel, or even tope, using lures. He then gave them a demonstration – and to their amusement brought to the surface another canvas bag! Unlike the first, though, this one was quite heavy. Intrigued, Ian delved inside. He was astonished to find several leather pouches in surprisingly good condition. Quickly, he opened them, only to discover they were full of jewellery, a hoard of diamonds, rings, necklaces, bracelets, bangles and much more. Ian couldn't believe his luck.

Ever the opportunist, Ian took the treasure to a jeweller in Edinburgh, an old Army chum, who bought the load for £25,000 with no questions asked. Ian was suddenly wealthy, and this windfall enabled the McCullough family to develop a visitor centre, and to secure the future of Skye as a world-renowned tourist destination.

The McCullough Centre, just outside Kyleakin on a height overlooking the sea, became a landmark, and a reminder that Skye is indeed a "Treasured Island".

Images

Len Maynard

Raymond Gideon watched the cloud as it hovered in front of the sun. Any minute now and it would pass, releasing the sun's rays to play on the golden thatched roof of the farmhouse. His Hasselblad was fixed securely to the tripod, a new back fitted, a fresh roll of film in place. He checked the Polaroid print again. The light was perfect, picking up the pointing on the brickwork, reflecting from the casement windows. The effect was exactly the one he wanted, and long experience had taught him patience. The art of good photography was that of capturing light, and the light on this crisp autumnal morning suited his subject perfectly.

The cloud drifted past, exposing the sun and, touched by the rays, the farmhouse came to life. He leant over the camera, checking focus, and depressed the plunger of the cable release, activating the shutter. The picture was his, captured and caged.

He rolled the film on and took several more at varying exposures, leaving nothing to chance. He knew he could sell this photograph several times over. There were magazine editors who would pay highly for his work, and this image was exactly what they wanted. A bucolic scene, romanticised, perfectly lit – wish fulfilment for their many readers who lived in grey, urban landscapes and fantasised about a rural lifestyle that for most of them was just a pipedream. It was a hungry market, and he'd built a career on providing the images to fuel those eager dreams.

He was so absorbed in his work that he was unaware he was no longer alone on the hillside. When she spoke, he visibly started.

'Sorry,' she said. 'I didn't mean to make you jump.'

She had her back to the sun and he squinted to get a better look at her. Tall and willowy, with a crisp white ribbon catching long chestnut hair in a ponytail. She was dressed in a riding outfit of tan jodhpurs, knee-length black boots, a hound's tooth jacket and a white shirt, fastened at the neck by a gold brooch in the form of two crossed riding crops.

'Kate Hammond,' she said, extending her hand. Her other hand was holding the reins of a bay thoroughbred that stood at her side, steam rising from its flanks.

He took the hand and shook it warmly. 'Raymond Gideon,' he said, moving round to get a better look at her face. She looked no more than thirty and was extremely pretty with ivory skin and deep brown eyes that regarded him with something close to amusement.

She looked past him, following the line of the camera. 'The house looks much better from up here,' she said. 'From here you can't see that the thatch needs renovating, and that the walls are so bad they soak up the rain like a sponge.'

'Is it yours, the house?'

She nodded. 'It's been in my family for years.'

'You don't mind?' he said, gesturing to the camera.

'Why should I mind? It's quite flattering you should want to photograph my home. Do many people mind?'

'You'd be surprised.'

She smiled. 'Tell me, do you do this for a living?'

'Yes and no; I have a studio in Melpham. My bread and butter work is portraiture and weddings. This...' He gestured to the landscape. 'This is artistic indulgence.'

'But it pays?'

'Sometimes it pays very well. But I'd do it even if it didn't.'

The horse shifted its hooves, eager to be on its way. 'I'm sorry,' she said. 'I'm disturbing you. I didn't mean to. I was just riding past and saw you perched up here on the hillside. I'm afraid curiosity got the better of me.' She placed the toe of her boot in the stirrup and mounted smoothly. The horse settled immediately under her weight. 'I must get on,' she said. 'It was nice meeting you.'

She pulled lightly on the reins and the horse's head came up. 'Perhaps you'll let me have a print of the photograph,' she said. 'I'll pay you, of course.'

Gideon smiled at her. 'Of course, but no payment; call it a gift. I'll bring you a copy when I've printed some up.'

'You're very kind.'

He shrugged the compliment away. 'Give me a couple of days,' he said.

'I will,' she said and dug her heels into the horse's flanks. 'Walk on, boy.'

He watched her go – every inch the experienced rider, back straight but relaxed, hands holding the reins lightly, all control coming from the gentle pressure of her long slender legs.

Almost from instinct he reached for his thirty-five millimetre and fired off a number of shots at her departing back. It was a shame he couldn't get a front view, but he doubted he would forget Kate Hammond in a hurry.

* * *

'Well, what do you think?' Gideon said to his assistant, Marie. She picked up the sheaf of photographs he'd dropped onto the desk in front of her and began leafing through them.

'Marvellous,' she said. 'Were all these taken on Sunday?'

'The majority of them. The light was perfect, as you can see.'

Marie Brennan's passion for photography was matched only by Gideon's, but he was much the better photographer. She'd been working with him for just over a year and he'd been impressed enough by her skills to let her take over the bulk of the routine work, which was fine by her as she had a love of portraiture. The weddings were a different matter, as she found such formal events quite stressful, the responsibility of getting three-dozen shots quickly and perfectly quite daunting. But she was here to learn, and to learn from a master.

'I like this one especially,' she said. She'd stopped at the image of the Hammond farmhouse and was examining it closely. 'Where did you take it?'

'Up on Melpham Tor. I'm just amazed I've never noticed the place before. I must have been up there a hundred times.'

She laid the photograph down on the desk and picked up a magnifying lens, studying the print closely, a frown slightly creasing her brow.

'Something wrong?' Gideon said, staring over her shoulder at the photograph.

'You had an audience when you took this one.'

His mind conjured up the face of Kate Hammond and he smiled. 'Yes,' he said. 'I know. But the question is, how did you?'

She glanced up at him. 'You can see him.'

'Him?' He leaned in closer.

'Third window along. It's pretty vague, but there's definitely someone looking back at you. Upper floor, third window along.'

He lifted the photo and scrutinised it with the lens. Marie was right. There was definitely someone standing at the window of the farmhouse.

'Dammit!' Gideon said. 'I hadn't noticed.' There was irritation in his voice.

'Does it matter?'

He gave her a pitying look. 'Of course it matters. The whole purpose of a shot like this is to present an image of a place that's impersonal, so that the viewer, coming across it in a magazine or book, can immediately transpose themselves into it... so they can imagine themselves living there. You can't do that if you have someone, perhaps the owner of the house, staring back at you. It shatters the illusion.' He dropped the photograph back on the desk with a snort of disgust. 'Bugger it!' he said.

He spent the rest of the morning with a family from the other side of town who'd commissioned him to shoot a series of portraits. The family was large with three children, both sets of grandparents and a King Charles spaniel. The adults were well behaved and took his direction without question. The children and the dog took more persuading. Normally it was the type of work he would have happily left in the capable hands of Marie, but she was tied up in the darkroom, processing films from a wedding the previous Saturday.

Throughout the morning he found his mind drifting back to the photograph of the farmhouse, and to the figure staring back at him from the upstairs window. He couldn't explain to himself why the image bothered him so much, but every time he pictured it in his mind his body gave an involuntary shudder.

The rest of the day was frustrating. He wanted to get into the darkroom and investigate the picture further, but a succession of customers kept him occupied until closing time. Marie left at five thirty and he pulled down the blinds and retreated to the darkroom.

Three hours later he was still there.

Finally he switched on the light and took the finished enlargements through to the office. He spread the pictures out on the desk and sat down in the chair. This time there was no need for a lens. He had a number of ten by eight inch images of the face that was staring back at him from the farmhouse. He picked up the sharpest picture and sat gazing at it, lost in thought, his hands shaking slightly as he focussed on the face.

The man in the picture looked about his age, mid-forties. The skin was pale, made paler by the jet-black hair that was swept away from his face. He didn't recognise him, but then he hadn't expected to. The eyes were dark, the face thin, but it was the expression on the man's face that made his hands tremble.

He had never in his life seen an expression of such stark terror as that on the man's face. There was terror, and something more; hopeless, abject despair.

It was the face of a man deeply frightened by something, and who had given up all hope of avoiding whatever terrified him.

With a low whistle he dropped the photograph to the desk and leaned back in his chair. There was a story here, a terrible story of human tragedy, captured for all time on photographic paper. What the story was he couldn't begin to imagine, but he knew that one way or another he would have to discover it.

He checked his watch. It was too late to do anything about it tonight, but first thing in the morning he would deliver the photographs of the farmhouse to Kate Hammond, and perhaps then he would discover what the story was.

He sorted through the images and found the best general shot of the farmhouse and slipped it into his attaché case, along with one of the enlargements, and then he scribbled a note to Marie. She had her own key and would open up the shop in the morning. The note was terse. *Delivering the photo of the farmhouse. I'll be in later. Hold the fort. Ray.*

He propped the note on the desk, and locked up for the night.

* * *

His route the next morning took him around the base of Melpham Tor, a twisting, circuitous lane bordered by high hedgerows obstructing the view of the fields and meadows beyond. At every junction he craned his neck, trying to see past the tall stands of hawthorn and cow parsley, looking for the Hammond farmhouse. It came upon him so suddenly he nearly missed it. Not the house itself, just a weather-beaten sign at the head of a narrow track. In faded white letters on a curling piece of plywood was the name 'Hammond'. He'd overshot the entrance by several yards before the sign registered. With a curse he checked his mirror, threw the car into reverse and backed up just past the track, then, spinning the wheel eased the car forward.

The track was badly overgrown, ferns and nettles crowding in from both sides, while long, whippy branches of bramble scraped against the car's paintwork. He followed the track for half a mile before coming up against a five-bar gate that cut the track in half.

He climbed out of the car and went to inspect the gate. Like the sign the gate was the worse for wear, the cross struts rotting and flaking wood. There was another, smaller sign affixed to the gate, but the letters had all but been obliterated.

Beyond the gate the track deteriorated into a wet and muddy morass, pot-holes and puddles, which surprised him as there hadn't been rain for weeks and the country was in the middle of a prolonged heat wave that had dried rivers and reduced the level in the local reservoir by half.

The track was in such a state that he doubted he would be able to drive any further. He went back to the car and locked it. He kept a pair of rubber over-shoes in the boot of his car – along with a spare camera they were a necessary part of his kit. He liked to think he was covered for every eventuality. Better to be over-prepared than to miss a shot. He slipped them on over his canvass espadrilles and went back to the gate.

He had to climb over as the gate was secured by a heavy chain and padlock, rusted through lack of use. He dropped down on the other side of the gate and started to pick his way carefully along the track.

In the distance he could see the Hammond farmhouse, as pristine and beautiful as it appeared in the photograph. As he got nearer he could see no damage to the thatch, and the walls looked as sound as they must have when they were first built, sometime back in the eighteenth century.

In front of the house was a cobbled courtyard and to the left of it a stable block, but there was no sign of horses. He wondered if Kate Hammond was out riding again, but when he tugged on the antiquated bell-pull a voice floated down to him from the upper floor. 'Won't keep you a moment.'

After a minute or so the door opened and Kate Hammond stood there smiling. 'Mr Gideon. Have you brought my photograph?'

Out of her riding clothes she looked completely different. She wore a floral print dress and her hair was swept up, dark curls piled on top of her head. The hair and the make-up she wore – deep red lipstick and rouge-blushed cheeks – gave her a strangely old-fashioned appearance, but she was as beautiful as he remembered and her smile was welcoming.

'I was just changing the beds,' she said by way of apology for keeping him waiting. 'Do come in.'

She led him through to an immaculately tidy sitting room occupied by an old-fashioned three-piece suite covered in faded chintz. The room itself seemed rooted in the past. Against one wall was a Welsh dresser, its shelves adorned with willow-pattern plates and a number of framed photographs, mostly black and white portraits. His eyes scanned them quickly and professionally. There was a picture of an elegant couple, the sepia tones softening the severity of the harsh Edwardian clothes they wore. To the right of this was a head and shoulders portrait of a handsome man in an RAF uniform, cap tilted at a rakish angle, a briar pipe clenched between neat white teeth. There were others but Kate Hammond was talking to him and he transferred his attention to her.

'...so good of you to take the trouble to deliver the photograph. I rarely get into town these days.'

'It was no trouble,' he said. 'Mind you, this place took some finding.'

She smiled. 'Off the beaten track,' she said. 'Geoffrey used to say it was the house's main attraction.'

'Geoffrey?'

'Sorry. I should have explained. Geoffrey was my husband. We moved here not long after we were married. Unfortunately he didn't live long enough to really get to enjoy the place.'

'I'm sorry,' Gideon said.

She waved the apology away. 'No reason to be. It was a long time ago, and we had a few very good years together.' She clapped her hands together like an excited child. 'Anyway, to the purpose of your visit.'

He unzipped the attaché case and handed her the photograph. Her eyes lit up as she gazed at it. 'But it's wonderful,' she said. 'You've really captured the spirit of the place. It's hard when you have lived in a house for so long, especially living alone, to see it as others do. This...' She clutched the photograph close to her breast. '...this makes me look at the house with fresh eyes.'

Gideon smiled at her enthusiasm, but a question still gnawed away at the back of his mind. He cleared his throat and brought the question to the forefront. 'I'm not sure your friend shares your pleasure at being photographed. He looks quite anxious.'

The smile dropped from her face to be replaced by a frown. 'Friend? Sorry, I'm not sure who you mean.'

He stood beside her. 'There,' he said, pointing to the third window along. 'I thought it must have been your husband, but of course that couldn't...'

She followed the line of his finger with her eyes. 'I still can't see...'

He reached into his case again, took out the enlargement of the face that had stared so forlornly at him.

Kate Hammond gave a cry of delight. 'But that's Marcus. Marcus Bannister. I thought he'd gone. I thought I'd lost him.' She took Gideon's arm and led him to a watercolour picture that hung from the wall. The painting was a skilled impression of the farmhouse, economic and deft brushwork lending the place an ambience missing from his photograph.

'I'm afraid I'm not quite with you,' he said. He could feel her fingers digging into the flesh of his forearm.

'But don't you see? If you took your photograph on Sunday it means Marcus is still here.'

'I still don't follow...' But she had moved away from him towards the stairs.

'He's upstairs!' she said, her voice rising in excitement. 'Oh you can't possibly realise what this means to me. Since Geoffrey died I've been so lonely, so terribly lonely.'

He watched as she ran up the stairs calling, 'Marcus! Marcus!' It was extraordinary behaviour. From above he heard the sound of doors being opened and closed, and every so often Kate Hammond's voice calling Marcus's name.

He turned back to the watercolour, studying the picture in more detail. It was a stylised image of the house, but none the worse for that. His gaze travelled on to the bottom right hand corner of the picture. The artist had signed it. *M. Bannister, 1955*. He looked closer but there was no mistake. The date was definitely 1955, over sixty years ago.

He had the sudden urge to leave the house. He walked back past the dresser and the photograph of the airman caught his eye again, only this time he saw the inscription. *To my Darling Kate. Your loving husband, Geoffrey.*

He stared hard at the photograph. When he'd first seen it he'd assumed it was a portrait of Kate Hammond's father. The photograph was old, slightly faded in its frame, and he could tell from the style of the portrait and the paper it was printed on that it couldn't have been taken within the last thirty years.

He lifted it from the shelf and turned it over. It was held in the frame by three small clips. He eased them to one side and removed the back plate. As he expected the photographer had stamped his name on the back of the photograph. It was a name that brought back memories of his childhood, growing up in Melpham. Lionel Wilson had his shop and studio in the High Street, nearly opposite to where Gideon's now stood, and as a boy he had spent long hours staring at Wilson's fine photography. A window filled with glowing visual testimonials to Wilson's craft. It was staring at these photographic masterpieces that had inspired his own passion, and prompted his continual nagging of his parents until they finally relented and bought him a small box camera of his own.

It was Lionel Wilson's name stamped on the back of the portrait of Geoffrey Hammond, and Gideon knew for a fact that Wilson had sold his shop and retired to Bournemouth in the early nineteen sixties, over fifty years ago.

Whatever was happening at the Hammond farmhouse Gideon wanted no part of it. He clipped the frame back together again and set it back on the dresser. He was at the front door when Kate Hammond appeared at the top of the stairs. 'It's no use... he's not here.'

He glanced up at her, said nothing but pulled open the door.

'But you can't go,' she said as she descended the stairs. 'It's so lonely here.'

He stepped outside and stopped dead.

Outside the landscape had changed. Outside *everything* had changed.

He stared at the trees surrounding the house. They stood, tall stiff sentinels, unmoving, their leaves and branches static. There was absolute silence, with not even the sound of a bird or the buzzing of a bee to disturb it. In a neighbouring field a tractor stood motionless, clods of earth thrown up by the plough it towed hanging in mid-air, whilst above the plough a flock of gulls were frozen in time, wings spread, beaks open, giving the impression of china models hung from wires.

He took a few tentative steps forward, and stopped again, but this time he stopped because he couldn't physically walk any further. He stretched out his hands and touched a flat, shiny surface covered with a two dimensional image of a landscape. A photograph of a landscape, huge and all encompassing. Slowly he turned back to the house. Kate Hammond stood in the doorway of the farmhouse, but she was shifting in and out of focus, as if he was looking at her through a heat-haze, or through an out of focus lens. Her lips were moving but the words were a long time reaching his ears.

'I said you couldn't leave.'

* * *

Marie read the note and dropped it back onto the desk. 'Thanks a bunch, Ray,' she muttered, but her irritation was tempered with unease. On her way to work that morning she'd finally worked out what was bothering her about the photograph Gideon had taken of the farmhouse. She was born and raised in Melpham and knew the town and its surroundings well, especially Melpham Tor. She'd played there as a child, and during her teenage years had spent much of her courting time on the green hill. She knew the tor and its surrounding landscape and knew there wasn't a house that matched the photograph Gideon had taken.

She went through to the darkroom and switched on the light. Gideon was an untidy worker and every flat surface was strewn with photographs. She lifted a pile from beside the developing tank and started to leaf through them, but the sound of the shop bell interrupted her.

A middle-aged couple were standing on the other side of the counter. The man smiled. 'Phillips,' he said. 'We have a nine thirty appointment with Mr Gideon.'

Marie smiled apologetically. 'I'm afraid Mr Gideon's been called away. I'm his assistant.'

'Are you a photographer?'

Marie nodded. 'Come this way,' she said and led them through to the studio.

It was late afternoon before she got another chance to enter the darkroom, but this time she found what she was looking for almost immediately. The negatives from the shot Gideon had taken on the Sunday were in an envelope buried under a pile of wedding proofs. She turned on the red light and started to work.

Back in the office she ran her hand through her short mousy hair and stared at the print in her hand. She'd printed the image of the Hammond farmhouse, but it was very different to the one Gideon had shown her the day before. This photograph showed the farmhouse, but it was a derelict wreck. Roof timbers showed through the collapsed thatch and on one side of the house the wall had fallen down, exposing a ramshackle and dilapidated interior.

She dropped the photograph to the desk, grabbed her camera and left the shop, locking the door behind her.

The sun was a fierce red ball hanging in the sky to the west as she took the lane that cut around the bottom of the tor. She parked under the shade of some trees and started to climb the hill. A few ramblers passed her on their way down to the bottom, looking at her curiously as she strode upwards, her mouth set in a thin determined line.

Two thirds of the way up, she shielded her eyes against the dying sun and looked about her. It was all so familiar, the view over the town, the plastics factory beyond it, blighting the landscape with its crude industrial architecture. Slowly she worked her way around to the other side of the tor where the scenery was mostly rural, a patchwork of fields, stripped bare now by the combine harvesters; raw earth ploughed into dusty furrows, separated from each other by green strips of hedgerow.

Through a gap in a line of poplar trees she saw the ruin. It was just as it appeared in the photograph she had printed earlier. A dilapidated building, deserted and unloved, awaiting the re-developers bulldozer. She fished in her camera bag and took from it a telephoto lens. She fixed it to the camera and raised it to her eye. Twisting the focus ring she brought the image of the farmhouse to crystal clarity. Then with a cry she dropped the camera. The strap caught the camera mid-fall and jerked against her neck, jarring it and making a friction burn on the soft skin of her nape.

Slowly she raised the camera to her eye once more.

There in the centre of the focusing screen was an image of the farmhouse, pristine, newly thatched, with stout, well-built walls and woodwork that looked freshly painted. When she took the camera away from her eye and looked past the row of poplars she saw the ruin again.

A thin bead of sweat trickled down her back and she shivered.

Back in her car she laid her camera on the passenger seat and gripped the steering wheel to stop her hands from shaking. What she'd seen was impossible. The rational part of her mind told her that over and over again. But a darker part of her mind urged her on. She started the car and eased out slowly onto the lane. Somehow she had to find Gideon. And there was only one place to look for him.

* * *

She found his car halfway along a rutted track blocked by a five-bar gate. In the russet glow of the fading sun she could just make out the outline of the house a quarter of a mile further on. She picked her way through the mud and potholes, following the path Gideon had taken earlier. By the time she reached the house her feet were soaked and her arms and legs were scratched and bleeding from countless thorn-sharp brambles that spilled out onto the overgrown path.

The house was as she'd seen it from the tor – a ruin of a building, ravaged by age and neglect. The door was hanging askew from one hinge. She pushed it to one side, peering into the gloomy interior. There was no sign of life, and certainly no sign that anyone had come through this way earlier.

Inside the short hallway the floor was littered with broken crockery and cracked tiles that had lifted from the concrete base beneath. She crunched over the remnants of a dinner service, trying to adjust her eyes to the gloom within.

'Gideon! Ray! Are you here?' She stopped, listening, but the house was silent. She pressed on past the rickety-looking staircase and on through to the downstairs rooms.

The first room she tried was empty, stripped back to the bare boards. Wallpaper peeled from the walls, once patterned with roses, now mottled with mould and scabbed with birdlime. There was a patch against one wall where a dresser once stood, the outline of it marked by a brightening of the paper where it had been protected from the sun's bleaching rays. A doorway led through to a large kitchen, but opportunists had stripped it. There was a large hearth and evidence that a range cooker had once stood there.

She shook her head sadly. She could almost picture what the house had been like, in happier times. Meals eaten around a large refectory table; laughter and conversation bubbling like the cooking pots on the range. Children perhaps, running in from the fields, spreading their muddy footprints on the terracotta tiles that made up the floor. It was really quite sad that a house could get to this state, and she felt for the people who had once considered this their home.

There was nothing here. No sign that Gideon had even come here.

Apart from his car, parked carelessly on the track.

She called again.

This time a sound answered her.

Above her head something scraped across the floor of one of the bedrooms.

She ran to the stairs. 'Gideon? Are you up there?' She tested the tread of the stair with her foot. The banister looked shaky but the risers appeared solid enough. She could imagine him coming here now. Perhaps he, like she, had decided to explore the place. Perhaps he'd had an accident. Maybe some floorboards had given way. Had he fallen and broken a leg or something? Was that him dragging himself across the bedroom floor?

'Oh, for Christ's sake, Gideon, answer me!'

She climbed the stairs gingerly, trying each step before settling her weight on it. If it should give way and she fell then they would both be marooned here. She couldn't imagine the place was much visited. It could be days before they were found.

She reached the top of the stairs and stopped on the landing. Ahead of her, at the end of the landing was a large rectangular window. The top rim of the setting sun could just be glimpsed, slipping slowly under the sill. She hadn't much time before it disappeared altogether, and she didn't want to be here in the dark.

To her right was one of the bedrooms, its door open and empty apart from a couple of wood pigeons that perched on the remnants of a chest of drawers. They watched her impassively, cooing softly as she walked past their room to the next.

The door to this room was closed. She tried the handle but the door wouldn't budge. 'Gideon? Ray, are you in there?'

She put her ear to the door.

Sobbing, a low, desolate sound, muffled by the stout oak of the door. She hammered on the door with her fist. 'Ray! What's happened?' She took two steps back and kicked at the door with the sole of her foot. The door shook in its frame but remained solid. She kicked again.

Slowly, with a groan of protesting timber, the door swung open.

The light that poured from the room was fierce; so fierce she threw up her hand to shield her eyes. It was like staring directly into the beam of a slide projector. Dust and debris from the room hung in the light, billowing like a mist, and through the debris something moved. Something with a black face, pale hair and brilliant white, piercing eyes. It was a man, moving slowly through the light towards her. It was a man she recognised as Raymond Gideon. But a negative image of Raymond Gideon, unformed, ill defined. He came towards her; his arms open for the embrace.

'So lonely. So terribly lonely,' he said as Marie started to scream.

My Station in Life

Diana Newson

'How would it be if I let everyone off Mrs?' said Mr Brandt, the rent collector, who haunted the factory rooms and tenements of the mill village of Stalybridge.

He leaned easily on the crumbling door frame, his top hat resting between his hands. Beyond the frame (there was no door) steps disappeared into the fetid darkness, and a stench of unwashed bodies and filth from the river breathed up on a current of sighs and groans.

I pulled my sister's dress closed against his gaze and briefly shut my eyes. I was dizzy from lack of food – our last meal had been a slurp of small beer and the end of a loaf yesterday. It was always like this, at month-end.

'We will pay, we get our wages tomorrow.'

My voice sounded disembodied even to my own ears. I should be asleep, my shift started again in two hours, and then I wouldn't be home for nearly a day. Beneath me I felt rather than heard them all turn in their sleep, some naked, sharing clothes like us, all stinking... like us. He had added, and added, and now there were fifteen people sharing the basement, and fifteen more working the overlapping shift. We were the lucky ones because at least the river rarely flooded the room when we were in it. When we slept, which is what we did there, our bodies filled the floor of that dank space and we all had to turn over together.

I wanted to protest that our rent should have decreased as more people were added, but he would simply have told me – us – to go if we didn't like it, and there was nowhere. We would have had to sleep in the gutter with cut-throats and rapists, in all weathers and seasons. At least here we had a roof, some friends who would look out for us, and public latrines only used by a hundred or so people. As I said to my sister, at least we're still alive. We were on the edge of starvation, disgraced and rejected, but had found our place here among the working people, who were too tired to care.

He smiled at me as I fought the weariness.

He knew we would pay...we went through this every month. The factory and the rent did not fit together, they were always one or sometimes two days adrift. He didn't even want my favours, I was too dirty and reeking for that. No, it was just to torture me, to keep me standing in the hot sun, to make me repeat the same words, and to show his power. I never let Cecilia talk to him. For one thing she was younger and prettier, and he might have overcome his distaste even though she was obviously with child. For another she had a temper and I couldn't trust her in word or deed. Mind you, even I briefly thought of plunging a knife into his splendid red neck. Not that I had a knife.

'Alright, a day's grace Mrs. I hope your wages will be sufficient, with fewer fines docked than last month.'

Actually, it was Cecilia who was fined - for sitting down whilst waiting for her next piece, when she thought the overseer's back was turned. Factory work was very hard on those almost birthing their child. The actual confinement was a black horror neither of us talked about. She would almost certainly lose her position at the factory for missing her shift. Pray her labour would be outside her shift so that she could get back to work with no one noticing. She'd already decided where to leave the babe, my niece or nephew. The nuns would clothe and feed, if the child survived the night on the doorstep, and most did.

He turned to go at last, but his fine boots slipped in the ordure and butcher's entrails in the street. He lost his balance and fell forward, with a splash, into the street's shit which lapped hungrily at his clothes. I could see he'd banged his head for he lay woozily, liquid filth bubbling at the corner of his mouth. A man could drown in the foot-deep mire, if someone didn't turn his head, and lift his mouth clear of the slime.

I was giddy with fatigue, my shift was due to start soon, and the screech of the factory klaxon would call us all to those grim gates. I turned away from the daylight and from Mr Brandt where he lay and stumbled down the dim steps to the basement room. My space had gone, and I had to wriggle between protesting bodies. Blessedly no longer upright, I quickly vanished into dreamless slumber.

* * *

At 4 in the afternoon the factory klaxon sounded. I awoke instantly, heart pounding and immediately started clawing my way up the basement steps, with everyone else. The fine for being late could be as much as a shilling and if I was fined, we would not cover our needs for this month. As I emerged, I blinked, eyes watering in the strong light. Ahead of me the chaser was chivvying the children. They were hard-faced and bleary-eyed, two of them not even dressed. He had a long whippy switch and was herding them down the street like livestock. The children were the worst for just falling back asleep.

I set my foot on the rutted pavement that swam above the mire. It was then I saw Mr Brandt. He hadn't drowned in the muck but was sitting in a doorway. I managed a slight curtsey in his direction and tried not to smile at the sight of his fine greatcoat encrusted with filth.

The sluts imprisoned in the nunnery would have a difficult time laundering that.

The factory gates loomed over me, black and spiked, like the gates of hell. A swarm of insects were coming out, among them my own Cecilia, dragging her bulk through the mud. We passed, and briefly embraced, although her eyes were half-closed, I think she was asleep already. I reached into her pocket and drew out the folded paper that held her month's wages, counting enough back in for her meal tonight. I murmured a brief warning about avoiding Mr Brandt if she saw him and then she was gone, stumbling in the direction of the privy, not the rented basement room. I winced at that, imagining her arriving after everyone else, and asking them to make way for her on the floor. Her size meant they'd have to squash even closer together. Also, her wandering in alone would make her vulnerable to the attentions of Mr Brandt – but I comforted myself that he hadn't looked at all well, but still clouded from his fall.

Walking towards those closed doors you could be forgiven for thinking that the very earth was trembling. It shook underfoot like the quaking of a virgin on her wedding night. It was caused by the mighty engines which powered the shafts on each floor, and woe betide you if you a rope caught you as it whistled past – I remembered the death of Iris Mayhew slammed against the ceiling and then the floor. Six revolutions had passed before the great indifferent violence was slowed and by then her screams had silenced. I tucked my hair more firmly into its bindings.

The doors opened, and a great wall of noise enveloped me. Now, no one spoke for nothing could be heard. Those workers who could leave their posts had already left, the others were doing their work with half an eye behind them waiting for their relief. My counterpart stood tending her shuttle, and I let her know I was there with a touched signal. She threw, and I caught, and she faded at the edges of my vision as she scuttled away. To eat, to visit the privy, to sleep. She'd be back tomorrow, like clockwork, and it would be my turn to sink gratefully out of sight.

* * *

I emerged the next morning after my shift, clutching a folded brown paper with my monthly wage. Over half of our combined wage would immediately go to Mr Brandt for a month's rent. The rest would be eked out for the month's food, but tonight, I would eat well, at the Inn. A whole quart of beer, meat pudding and broth, with plenty of bread to mop up. I looked around for Cecilia, my darling Cecilia, and she was nowhere to be seen. I should have passed her by now – she had one of those posts that could be left for a few moments as the workers changed shifts, so she was often there before I was allowed to leave. A sharp fear tore through my tiredness. Maybe it was her Time?

Then I saw him – Mr Brandt.

He stood by the factory gate and my Cecilia was at his side. There seemed no change to her except her dark eyes were even more huge. She was by him willingly, no restraint was being used, and he was no longer covered with dried excrement from the street. I approached, my hand clutching our wages in my pocket, so that if he demanded money I could give it to him. To my unease he was smiling – an expression I'd never seen on his face – and it made him look even more fearsome.

'It's your lucky day Mrs,' he said.

I looked mutely to Cecilia for an explanation, but her eyes were down-cast and I was forced to turn my regard to him again.

'Your sister found me in the street where I had fallen and offered me a mouth of water.'

The jag of fear sliced through me again, when would Cecelia learn to obey me, and avoid these hazards?

'I found I knew her,' he continued.

The world rocked on its axis, and not just because my head was swimming with exhaustion.

'In return for her kindness,' he continued, 'A month's free rent.'

My astonishment was great. Mr Brandt broke into a little-used laugh.

'And a free shift for her, to give her time to take the babe to the nuns.'

He tipped his still-muddy hat, more to Cecilia than to me, and laughed once more at the incredulity on my face. Then he turned and carefully made his way down one of the alleys leading away from the factory gates.

The blow to his head must have been serious indeed to induce smiling and laughing, I thought bitterly. I turned to my sister.

'Where is the baby now?' I asked. In reply she leaned forward, and I saw the babe nuzzling her breast, hidden in the folds of her clothes.

'We'll take it to the nuns. And call at the Inn on our return.' I said.

She sighed dreamily, and I knew I had to separate mother and child urgently, or our situation would become untenable.

'I suppose I must leave him with the nuns,' she said.

'Will you call him Albert like you wanted?' I said to distract her, as I took her free arm and started to walk towards the grimy Abbey.

'I thought I would name him for Mr Brandt,' she said. 'So that's just Brandt, as I don't know his Christian name.'

'That's not a real name...' I began, and then, because I knew the nuns would just rename the babe anyway, I smiled at her.

'Brandt it is.' I said.

Although in my mind the name Brandt was scored jaggedly, again and again, into a murderous curse.

The Sound of Silence

Emma Branch

Yes, if I press my ear to the door I can definitely hear it. Faintly at first. Then more insistently.

Scratch, scratch, scratch. As soon as I turn the handle.

Silence.

The room is empty apart from half a dozen unpacked packing cases, a deep chill and an unnerving feeling that I'm not alone. The sensible voice in my head asks calmly 'What's the worst a mouse could do to you?' All the other voices scream, 'Get out whilst you can.' I walk hurriedly back onto the landing, slamming the door hastily behind me. I tentatively rest my ear back against the door. Scratch, scratch, scratch.

I see no evidence of his being there. No nibbled boxes or mouse droppings. Just the noise and a dank sweet aroma that's like nothing I've smelt before. A humane trap failed to lure him, the snapping kind missed its mark. Nothing tempted him. Cheese, chocolate, fruit cake, a block of blue rat poison, all left untouched but still scratch, scratch, scratch.

I let my little intruder invade my head. Not a day went by when I didn't plot or plan his demise. He became my main topic of conversation, the worry that kept me from sleep. I lie awake straining my ears to hear him. Covering my ears to block out the sound. Scratch, scratch, scratch. When finally I slept I dreamt he was scampering over me, sharp little claws scratching at my face, bony paws tangled in my hair. I woke with a start. 'Enough,' I shouted into the cool quiet.

I invited a friend and his spaniel to tea. No coincidence, Ben was a Copper and Bess a retired sniffer dog. My hopes sank as she begged eagerly for cake and snoozed by the glowing fire. After a comfort break in my daffodils Bess dashed along the landing whilst Ben and I tiptoed along behind. We paused outside the door, ears pressed against the wood. Yes there it was. Scratch, scratch, scratch. Bess dashed in as the door swung open. She methodically swept backwards and forwards across the room. Standing on her hind legs to fill her nose with scent on top of the boxes. She scanned the various traps, nothing caught her attention. As I began to lose hope she sat down sharply by the little built in cupboard at the back of the room. She looked at Ben and back at the door, back to Ben with a gentle wag of her tail and then intently back at the door. 'That's it,' he announced, 'She's indicating.'

I told him the cupboard was empty. It wasn't deep enough even to store the boxes, nothing inside of interest to a mouse. Bess was sent out of the room and made to sit forlornly on the landing. Ben took the broom I'd been grasping and waved to me to open the cupboard slowly. As I lifted the latch the hinge squealed in protest, my heart pounded, cold sweat beaded along my spine. I expected a torrent of mice to tumble out, rolling like a wave across the floorboards. Nothing rushed out, only a cold draught and that intense sickly smell. Bess darted in, all good police dog procedure forgotten. Her nose busy in the far corner of the cupboard. Ben covered his face with his hand. 'Jeezz, I think your little friend crawled in here and died.' I reminded him that wasn't possible, we'd heard him only a few minutes earlier when we stood in the landing. The plaster board was damp and stained where it met the floor boards. I imagined I could hear it again now, more insistent than before, more determined to get out. *Scratch, scratch, scratch.*

I searched in the boxes and found a claw hammer and a screw driver. Together we prized the nails free. There wasn't enough room for Ben inside the cupboard so I elbowed him out of the way triumphantly yanking the edge of the board to bring an end to all these weeks of worry and stress. The board suddenly snapped free of its frame throwing me backwards in a slow-motion arc of plasterboard, cobwebs and dust. I watched frame by frame as a dried corpse swung free from her tomb, hair and ragged clothing streaming out behind her like a banner. I felt my breath crash out of my chest as I hit the floor. I felt the dry bones crash into me as she fell into my outstretched arms. Her sharp nails scratched my face, her bony fingers tangled in my hair.

My face contorted to match her silent scream. No noise came from me, I lay frozen in fear. The only sound to be heard was a faint scratch, scratch, scratch as her jagged nails met the bare floorboards.

A Kitten Christmas

Marjorie Allwood

Mother cleaned behind my ears, but as I tried to wriggle away, a big heavy paw descended upon me.

'It's the same every year. Every year it happens,' said Auntie Fay, the owner of the big heavy paw. 'A great big bird we're not allowed anywhere near, and the whole family running around wrapping things in shiny papers. It's the same every year.'

When I was cleaned to Mother's satisfaction, the paw was lifted, and I was allowed back into the basket, which I shared with Mother, Ben our older brother and Tabi, our sister. Ben and I were black and white like Mum, whilst Tabi was mostly ginger and white just like dad who lived around the corner.

'Still,' Auntie Fay continued, 'We do get some wonderful treats after they have opened the papers and boxes, so I can't complain.

Mother nodded, 'It's the same here, and the family's children get so excited. For that one night of the year, we can't get the kittens to go to sleep.'

'Herbert loves that bird,' Auntie May mused, 'Cooked or uncooked. I like the lights too, but we have remember that the tree is not meant for us to climb. Herb got himself stuck in it one year, fused all the lights and suffered an electric shock. My dear, I was mortified. It was some time before either of us was allowed in the lounge again.'

Auntie Fay and Uncle Herbert lived in another house around a bend in the close. Both were big, older tabby cats with no kittens of their own. So, Auntie Fay often came round to help mum and have a chat. I heard the cat flap and knew Dad was coming in. Dad lived in the next house to us and visited often. Now, he and Mum nuzzled, licked one another, and then, went to sit over by the Christmas tree, whilst we kittens went to sleep in the basket, with its warm paw print blanket.

* * *

In the close, you humans are known as 'the family'. Auntie Fay and Uncle Herbert, lived with an old couple whose children had long grown up and left their basket. Of course they were back here for the Christmas Holidays, now, with children of their own. As we kittens slept, the cats of the close met in 'the fields' an area of common land that led into the southern hills with high field village beyond.

Towards the northern area of the fields were the 'old woods' a place that nobody ever seemed to think about, although they had been there as long as anyone could remember. No one, if you asked around, had ever entered, or seen anyone else enter the old woods and, strangest of all, no children ever went to play there.

The adult cats sat around gossiping about many things, like how mice seemed too cheeky and intelligent nowadays for their own good. Christmases past, present and, very important, the recent improvements to a particular brand of cat food. When, who should arrive but, Auntie Maisie, a white cat with huge blue eyes, and Uncle Sergei, a Russian blue. They lived next door to each other at the upper end of the close. Now, Auntie Maisie loved nothing more than dressing up in jewelry and, with a ring on the tip of her tail, both she and Uncle Sergei went out with friends to cat parties. They both loved their lives and their respective owners.

The circle now livened up with purrs, meows, and other sounds filling the air until, tired, the group drifted off to their respective homes to wait for the night's magic to unfold.

A pale circle of silvery moon lent a faint luminosity to the tops of the trees and houses. Silence now reigned in the close. But there were some with other ideas!

* * *

It was after midnight when Auntie Maisie awoke. Usually she stretched and purred for a few moments on the luxurious rug she always slept on, but not tonight. Tonight she was certain that something was wrong. She slept in the children's room, and they were all sound asleep. But still, she felt something was wrong. Sensing the air, she left the room and went up the back stairs to where the family's old widowed grandmother lived in her small flat.

The bedroom door was open and two men in masks were menacing the old lady. For a few seconds Auntie Masie observed the men's movements then she took off out of her own cat flap, and through into ours. Auntie Maisie was owned by the grandmother, and often wore her jewelry. The old lady doted on her and bought her treats. She, in turn, loved the old lady. Mother was asleep with us in the basket when Auntie Maisie shot through the cat flap. Now, shocked and awake, she listened as Auntie Maisie explained what was happening next door. 'Oh, we really must do something,' said Mother. By now we kittens were awake and we quickly understood what was happening.

'Ben,' said mother, 'Go and alert Jock. Ask him to warn all the families that something is wrong.'

Jock was the old Scottie dog who lived two houses away from us. He had his own dog door and was always friendly to the cats of the close. He was an old dog and usually very quiet, but not on this night!

When Ben left, Mother turned to us. 'You two, go and tell your Auntie Fay and Uncle Herbert what is happening. We need their help.'

We were both still too small to climb through the cat flap, so Mother and Auntie Maisie helped push us through. Swiftly, we sped towards their house. I climbed on Tabi to get through their cat flap and then I helped haul her through. Soon all four of us were racing towards Auntie Maisie's house. We could hear Jock barking and scratching at the front door. Lights were coming on in windows, and doors were opening in the close as we raced towards the old lady's flat. Mother, Auntie Masie and Dad were already in the flat and we all joined them in the bedroom.

* * *

Well it was no contest; no contest at all. Two men in dark clothing, both with knives, desperately trying not to lose their eyesight or the, by now, torn balaclavas. Uncle Sergei using all four paws and claws, his back paws just a blur! With mum and dad also swinging and clawing the man's head, while the same thing was happening to the other one. Uncle Herbert, Auntie Fay, and Auntie Maisie were swinging and clawing wildly at eyes, ears and, noses. Those balaclavas were so helpful. The adult cats used them to hold on to their prey, while the men now couldn't see anything.

Jock was nipping at any ankle that came available while we kittens sat and watched. When the police arrived both men were well and truly beaten. The three officers were open-mouthed at the sight.

'Cuff them,' snapped the sergeant, finding presence of mind. 'Well, well, well, what have we here? Been playing with the little kitties have we?' The old, seasoned sergeant asked.

An ambulance arrived to take the shocked old lady to hospital. Luckily she was not seriously hurt and was able to return home in time for Christmas dinner and the Queen's speech. The two would-be burglars were also given first aid.

'Come with us,' the pretty police lady said. 'We've a lovely cell waiting. Can't guarantee Father Christmas though.'

The other two policemen fell about laughing. And so, off they all went. Well everyone was so excited, we kittens had to be almost held in our basket. Then gradually, a soft energy seemed to pervade the whole close. The families went back to their respective homes, and we cats fell fast asleep. So, no one saw the silvery mist descend out of the sky, hear the gentle tinkling of bells, or see the soft lights flitting from house to house. Nor did anyone see the lights and the mist coalesce, and ascend, back to the starry heavens.

In the morning there were presents everywhere and, it was not just cat food for us and dog food for Jock. Smoked salmon, turkey and, after Christmas, Jock had a tartan collar with a tiny real diamond! We cats were now loved by our owners more and more. Auntie Maisie and Uncle Sergei were both given new blankets with their names on. Auntie Maisie had a lovely jeweled collar and cat lead from her grateful owner. We kittens were stroked and loved by the children and given tiny little jeweled collars, as were our parents, Uncle Herbert and Auntie Fay. People started calling the close 'Christmas Close' and while the postal address didn't alter, the name tended to stick.

Christmas will be here again soon I wonder what, if anything might happen this year?

My sister's child

Diana Newson

Your Nanna is a fairy botanist
And you can learn Gardening off her.
Once a week you learn Gardening
At your Nanna's house.
She rattles in the shards, squeezes the black
     compost,
Scatters blue slug pellets,
which is where you come in.
"Slug-man" she calls you, with no irony.
"Where's my slug-man? A *small* shake. Enough!
     Enough!"

You're four years old right now,
And in the cross-hairs of all our loves,
You could spontaneously burst into flame.

"We need another one." she says to me firmly,
As if it's just a question
Of getting one Potted Up.

Out of the Earth

David Strong

'I'm not sure what I have found here, but it's very unusual,' I said, talking on the land line to the dig director in New York. As usual, the Irkutsk office was chilly and I was pacing up and down both in an attempt to get warm and with building excitement. We called it our office but it was really nothing more than a rented desk with wi-fi and communications, a photocopier and tea and coffee facilities. This was Siberia; people used to be sent out here by the KGB as a punishment. We did not expect modern, plush centrally heated offices.

This was to be our third year uncovering and documenting a family group of woolly mammoths that had been discovered by chance by a forester after a particularly heavy storm had caused a landslide and had left a point of a tusk poking out of the sodden ground. The excavation site was out in the middle of nowhere, surrounded by more nowhere, and trees, lots of trees: spruce, larch, pine, silver birch; but we were not interested in our current natural environment, we were archaeologists.

We had just re-opened the dig after the Winter recess when temperatures at the site rarely rose above -20. It would have been impossible to continue working during the cold months so we had packed everything away carefully; prepared, covered and protected and concealed the site – it was in little danger over Winter – after all it had been there for tens of thousands of years, so we left it to all intents and purposes as we had found it. Hidden. We left nothing of value over the Winter recess, let's face it, all we really left was a pile of old bones – the tusks may have been of value to grave-digging Japanese entrepreneurs who would grind mammoth tusks to dust and sell the dust as an aphrodisiac or as a cure for cancer. Ridiculous! But the site was secret and so far from anywhere that it was safe to leave.

There were usually two of us working on the dig, myself, Connor Stephens, 31 year old Smithsonian graduate with thirteen years archaeological hands on experience and Tom Martin who came over for a few weeks during the season to help, he was older than me and more experienced but less qualified. We did not talk much, no late night drinking sessions, no field girls to play around with. We enjoyed the tranquillity and the work. It engrossed us. Occasionally a student or two would join us; they would have to source their own funding, but serious work experience on an anthropological dig was hard to come by – and we welcomed the help and the company if it came free – and they could get here. Our local contact and Russian archaeological representative was a consultant from Irkutsk called Mahrat and he tended just to turn up when he was in the area. It was through him that we had the visas and permits to be working in Siberia, without him none of the work could have started or continued. It was Mahrat who had first recommended the site for excavation after some interesting bones had been uncovered back in 2009.

The ground had thawed rapidly after we had put the tents and canvas up and the heaters on. We'd cleared away the top soil and that had been laid back down in October and we had made a good start to the season.

'No, the mastodon bones are as we left them. The family group is exactly as we left it and undisturbed. But I have made significant progress on the bull, the separate specimen. The main frame is wonderfully presented but there's something else there, something more elaborate, more complex remains within the bull, it's a mystery and I am after a second opinion.'

'Connor, you mean you need more money,' George replied.

'George, I am not one of those field workers that is always phoning you up and begging for more resources. You know how cheaply we run this dig – I sleep in my motorhome for months on end and this office probably only costs you a few hundred roubles a month,' Connor complained.

'So you don't want any more money?'

'I'll e-mail you some shots so you can see where we are and what we have found. I have lifted out all the spoil, put up the grid and taken some really neat overhead pictures, but I'm confused. I just need to invite a guy, Patrick Tiler, I met a couple of years ago in Maine…'

'And he wants expenses. I knew you wanted money, that's all you people ever call me for… George I need more machinery, George, we want to extend the dig time…' I deliberately remained calm and did not rise to his taunts. George could be bombastic but I knew that I had his attention.

'He'll be interested, and won't need a consulting fee. I only need to pay for his flight and car hire'.

We had backing from Yale and The Smithsonian but the funding was always finite and always an issue. George was our director and had to answer to the committee made up of sponsors.

'What have you found?'

'I don't know, but I need a second opinion. It is ground-breaking stuff, George. You know I wouldn't be asking if I was in doubt.'

'OK, tell him to invoice us. But no first class and no Merc.'

George put the phone down on me without a goodbye. I punched the air.

* * *

The dig needed more funding. What anthropomorphic archaeological dig did not? But we were at the boring edge of archaeology, a group of mammoths caught in a sudden arctic storm and buried in snow only to be discovered 25000 years later did not have the same romantic attraction as dinosaurs... big dinosaurs like those that had been found in Patagonia.

25000 years ago the part of Siberia we had been working in had been very different. It had been a prairie, a vast grass plain that in the Summer was verdant and lush. Mammoths roamed freely and in small herds, moving with the seasons and travelling up to a thousand miles annually. They were family groups of 10/12m a dominant bull and a small group of cows and adolescents, they had few predators, the calves were occasionally taken by a tiger or wolf pack but even the adolescents had little to fear. The male mammoth had tusks that could be three meters and more and were flamboyantly and magnificently curled up, the mammoths were all covered in a thick matted fur that protected them from the ferocious winters that could descend so quickly in this part of the world. They must have been majestic beasts to see, often half as big again as the biggest elephants we have in Africa or India – it was conjectured that the bulls trumpet could be heard from over a mile away.

There was what looked like a tail. About six feet long and it looked prehensile. The main body was some four feet long with strong legs, the head was almost bird-like, with a strange pointed structure. I had immediately thought of an ostrich like animal, or a kangaroo with the bones broken, contorted and twisted and compressed and that the timeline would be totally thousands of years different. Just a coincidence that glacial movement or subsidence had slid them together. But, the whole thing appeared to be in a scrunched up foetal position, all wrapped up. It only added to the confusion. A kangaroo in the Russian steppes? A kangaroo from 25000 years ago? Its descendants only to be found in Australasia? Had I found a new species? That was ridiculous. You do not find only one specimen and there was no precedent. Perhaps there was something I was missing, perhaps it was just a large female and not a male and I was just looking at a malformed pregnancy, perhaps there had been ongoing tree root disturbance and movement. But it by far was the most interesting and exciting discovery I had come across in my thirteen years, each day was a joy, each moment of uncovering, brushing, revealing was totally involving. I knew from the very first moment that I had something special and I savoured it.

* * *

Patrick arrived a week later. It had rained constantly for days and I had not really had much opportunity to scrape and reveal anything further. Even with the canvas up it was impossible to work, the forest ground was saturated, the rain ran in rivulets, I spent more time bailing out the pit and trying to keep the bones as dry as I could. It was constantly dusk, miserable and wet. My enthusiasm was dampened too: it was good to see a dry and friendly face.

'You didn't tell me about the road,' Patrick said.

'Ah. There isn't one.'

'Nor the mobile phone coverage. My satnav had no idea where I was.'

'No. I know. Hope the map helped,' I said.

'The hand drawn map...'

'And you saw the signs off the Irkutsk road onto the Bratsk track...'

'Yep. And I took them down as I came past. You're being secretive Connor, that's unlike you.'

There was a moment of hand shaking and back slapping and I put the kettle on. I was desperate for Patrick to arrive so that I could share mine and Tom's discovery. We were beginning to imagine all sorts of Darwinian answers.

* * *

'I don't know.' Patrick said, looking down in the pit from the side.

'Neither do we. Should we expand the site, we could open up several more pits?'

The rain had passed and we had spent a couple of days drying out the dig and shoring up the sides to make it safe from collapse.

'I think it might come to that. But you'll have to do it by hand, they'd never pay for a digger to come all the way out here.'

The pit was six meters by four and contained a mass of bones, a convoluted confusing mass of bones that had turned to rock. We had found eight distinct specimens that had presumably huddled and perished together in the frozen mud – it was nearly impossible to distinguish one specimen from another, cow to calf, adolescent to calf. We had lifted out and separated a mother and a calf, catalogued and labelled and crated it up ready for transport but there was still so much more work to do. And we had to sort out an answer to our riddle. What was it?

We sent samples of the bones off for Carbon 14 dating. Urgent.

Tom, Patrick and I had made the journey to the Irkutsk office to phone up the lab in Maine for the dating results of the bone sample we had carefully scratched from both the bull and the unborn malformed infant. We had moved neither specimen but had managed to clear away some of the overlaying adolescent bones that had obscured the bull. It had been a painstaking work, photographing every stage as we went, we had also extended the pit a foot to the left to see if there was anything else we had not discovered.

'You playing games with me Connor?'

'No.'

'These samples you sent me. 25k old mammoth. Fine. C14 puts it at the right period. But there's too much of an anomaly in the unborn infant samples. The reading is not right. You probably have contaminated it. It goes way off piste – like 80,000 years. It's not right, the carbon residue is not balanced, we've had the calcium levels checked and they are wrong too – you sure you've taken a bone sample and not just a scraping from the bottom of your boot?' he sarcastically asked.

'Absolutely certain. And we labelled and sent the samples in an airtight pack – they cannot, 100 per cent be contaminated.'

'Sorry buddy. If you're not playing games someone is... the sample you sent me is not prehistoric bone.'

I felt light headed. My heart was beating wildly. Why me? Why had this fateful thing landed in my lap? And was I about to make a fool of myself by declaring that the Loch Ness Monster had been found or that fairies were for real or yeti were actually abominable?

* * *

We closed up the dig early. And were absolutely thorough in the dismantling. We protected, covered, layered and put the spoil back in shovel by shovel. We removed all signs of the excavation, literally covered our own tracks. George had increased our funding to allow two assistants to join us a month previously, they had to pay for their own flights and transport but were offered a bursary. We also had a cameraman who documented what we were doing. We removed the bull and unborn infant and rented a bare warehouse in Irkutsk, ready to reassemble the jigsaw pieces and display the remains as they had been seen in situ. It took ages to organise and we had Russian advisors and military crawling all around. Mahrat came over daily. But we kept our findings to ourselves, this was going to be our moment.

We had thought long and hard about how to present our findings.

George had come over, along with two representatives from the funding committee plus a Smithsonian guy. There were two elderly Russian specialists a uniformed Russian man who looked like he could be KGB but was really friendly and jovial and a few other invited anthropologists and palaeontologists. A few trusted members of the press. And a camera crew. This was news. Old news maybe, boring mammoth news perhaps, not even exciting tyrannosaurus or velociraptor news.

You could not call it a press conference. More an open meeting for open minded, like minded invited enthusiasts. There were few amenities offered in the warehouse, a few tubular chairs, tea and coffee and fixed floodlighting showing a reconstructed dig. There were a mass of bones, protruding rocks in shapes and lines. It was not easy to make out without a trained eye.

I stood in front of all and with a stick pointed to the pit and started to explain:

'Gentlemen. This is our dig. We have relocated here because the actual dig is in the middle of a forest, in the middle of nowhere North of here. The Russian authorities would not allow us to move any more of the specimens, they are all to stay in Siberia but we will be allowed to continue our work under the supervision and guidance of the Russian archaeological authorities. We are indebted to them for their help and support. This is their find, their property.' I looked about me and knew that I had them, they were hanging on my every word.

'25000 years ago this family of mammoths got caught in a mother of a Winter storm. Six feet of snow can fall in a day out here. And they all perished together. The peat and the sediment preserve the bones. Nothing has been altered, this is exactly, precisely as we found it. We have comprehensive data and video footage. But, we need help. We need the best, the world experts.'

I pointed with a stick: 'This specimen here is the bull, the largest mammoth and the principal. You can see the frame of something underneath, and within the main set of bones'   I pointed and explained the curvature of spine.... explained that it looked like a baby within the main body... or as if an animal had pushed out the guts and organs and had climbed inside the dying body to escape the -40C cold....

'And here's the point guys....' I hesitated and waited, swallowing, my voice wavering with nerves. 'It's unlike anything I have ever seen. It fails all the tests. I think it is off world. An alien.'

There was a silence. You could have heard a pin drop.

Rebirth

Erol Hasan

When Sarah died, you thought you could not live on. Then, when you got the diagnosis of cancer, you did not expect to last long, anyway. You could have given up. But you kept going; you hung in; in spite of the morbid way you were talking, and the wretched way you looked (no offence intended, you understand).

And you are here today, five years on. Sheila is the spark in your life. She does not remind me of Sarah, who was very effervescent, extravert and (excuse me) sexy. Sheila is very demure, modest, undemanding and thoughtful. I have often wondered what she said to you at the wake following Sarah's funeral. Something switched in you. The stress seemed to drain out of you. You became accepting, and you acquired a quiet courage.

You do not see as much of your family, these days. What happened with your brother Derek? I noticed some irritation between the two of you at the wake. He seemed to be chastising you. A couple of minutes before that, you had disappeared to the toilet, a bit unexpectedly. Did he catch you breaking down? Your family are very conscious of their image, forgive me for saying.

I must say, you seem very content these days. You do less, but enjoy what you do more. You appear to live for yourself and your partner, not for the audience of your family and social circle. And, speaking of friends, you see fewer people these days, and your association is not frivolous. Dare I say that you used to be conscious of who you were seen with, what you were seen doing (usually drinking and flirting), and how much wealth you were able to flaunt?

If I am honest, you and Sheila are as if you were stuck to one another with glue. You and Sarah were as if the two of you were attached to a wide circle of people. Am I being unfair? And now you are content with walking every day, rather than thrashing your body – and sometimes your opponent's- on the squash court. I expect that is because of the illness. It is understandable.

You still teach, but no longer in a school. Have you lost your principles? Or do you just prefer the tranquility of private tutorial work? Sarah wouldn't have approved. I bet your family don't.

And what made you change from Church of England to Methodist? Sheila, of course. This is the hardest one to get my head around. You bury your beloved Sarah in one church, and then start attending a place of worship with a different philosophy. You go from champagne socialist to socially conscious ... You're making me dizzy!

I am pleased to see that you are playing the piano again. And singing. You make less noise now, and sound better for it. You seem more relaxed, and spiritually at ease. You don't look like you're trying to impress anyone.

Yours sincerely,
Your alter ego

* * *

Thank you for your words of advice. I have changed. Anyone would, if they were to go through a double trauma like I did. I take on board your comparison of Sarah and Sheila. You obviously spend a lot of time thinking about the women in my life.

What I had with Sarah, and now with Sheila, have nothing to do with one another. We are talking about two very different periods in my life. When Sarah passed away, my life changed. In a sense I was reborn; I shall explain.

Sarah was not a frivolous person. She was bubbly, and fun-loving, but caring and deeply sensitive. If you are going to make comments, you should look a little beneath the surface. I loved her external and internal self. I still do.

Sheila is also very sensitive. It is her external self that is very different. She is right for me as I am now.

It is true that Sheila bided her time, and took her opportunity. You could argue that she was a little hasty, approaching me so soon after Sarah's death. But she sensed that the time was right for me; that I needed lifting; that my mood could have deteriorated quickly. And don't be shocked that the first move came from Sheila. It was very guarded, thoughtful and respectful. She and Sarah had been friends; there was nothing predatory about her behaviour. She simply tapped me on the arm, said she was sorry and offered to talk to me. She showed me a laminated poem she had picked up in her local church (our place of worship now). It went as follows:

Lord, let me be true to myself,
And to the abilities that you have given me;
Give me faith and courage,
Whatever life brings;
And let me experience hope
At all times, and at all stages
Of my life;
What is more,
Maintain my capacity for love;
In spite of loss and disillusionment,
Let me be generous in love,
In its myriad forms and manifestations.

I also found this, myself:
Lord, though my body is no more,
My soul lives on;
And this life is what it is;
A preparation for life beyond;
And love has no endpoint,
And no boundary, no limit;

What is precious in this life
Is still valued hereafter,
But what is worthy of love
Is multifarious.

Don returned to his sofa, and soon he was asleep.

"It's OK, you know it is. I am here now, and I am happy. I always knew that one day you and Sheila would be together. It made sense. Thank you for putting up with the partying, and with my, sometimes, wild behaviour."

"But you know I loved you; I still do..."

"Yes, of course; it's O.K."

Sarah's face vanished, and Don woke up. It was a dream, but was it more than that? Sarah was fine (in a new life, and happy), or was it just his own mind providing catharsis for him.

* * *

When Sheila arrived, he greeted her, then sat quietly.

Eventually, she enquired, "Are you alright?"

"Yes; well, I was just thinking, well..."

"About Sarah. I thought we'd been through all that."

"Yes, I know we have, but..."

"You were with her for a very long time; it is inevitable. A part of you probably still loves her. That just makes you sincere. I would not be with you, if I did not understand and accept that."

* * *

The following day, there was a solemn atmosphere at church.

The minister announced, "I am very sad to inform you of the passing of George Mellor. He was a good man, and is no doubt at peace, to be joined one day by his loving wife, Julie."

Sheila squeezed Don's hand.

A Monstrous Mother Murderer

Sheila Molloy

Sarah planned to kill her mother next time she saw her. She had several options worked out and was pretty sure she could get away with it. What worried her most was all the play-acting she'd have to engage in afterwards. Repressing the urge to confess. Lying to the kids.

She had never murdered anyone. Not a human anyway. Only the dog. And even then she paid a vet to end his life. Five years on and she still felt guilty. And this was her mother. There was even a dedicated word for it - matricide - which was a clue about how seriously society viewed breaking such a taboo. Sarah imagined herself strip-searched, given scratchy clothing and the cell door clanging shut behind her.

'What you in for, then? a burly woman covered in tattoos would ask as she swung herself down from the top bunk before browsing Sarah's body.

'Killing my mother.'

That probably merited a pretty low status in the prison hierarchy. Sarah might have to be incarcerated in a special wing for her own protection. And what a gift for headline writers: 'Monstrous Mother Murderer – cruel counsellor showed no mercy, a court heard.'

Sarah's training taught her that when you're a child, synaptic pruning takes place. Cerebral secateurs carefully snip away the dead wood – skills someone is never likely to need and will never miss. Two years ago they began to run amok in her mother's brain. The veins that carried the blood supply fuelling cognition narrowed and the blades began stripping away memories. They started work with the twig memories, cutting them off before they sprouted leaves which could blossom into friendships and also ruthlessly severed links between action and intent. Sarah's mother struggled to recall the new milkman's name or she would go into a room and wonder why she was there.

'It's just forgetfulness – happens to everyone,' Sarah assured her.

Sarah only realised how serious it was when the secateurs burrowed deeper and the late night phone calls began.

'It's John, your mother's neighbour. She's turned up here again.'

Bruises appeared on her mother's face and arms which she could not explain. Now the blades were attacking the bigger branches, hacking away knowledge at the heart of identity. Off came the meaningful relationships, recognition of people her mother once cherished, and all her vocabulary. Also consigned to the lost memory mix went social skills she mastered before the age of five. Like forgetting that the build-up of pressure in the bowel was a prelude to pooing your pants. Or that it was necessary to hold a spoonful of soup horizontally as it made its way to your mouth to prevent soiling your clothes. Now her mother, who had always looked so smart, had blouses resembling an oil painter's palette – tea and tomato soup, globules of porridge, bits of soggy biscuit. The secateurs had now almost cut through to the thick trunk of meaningful recall where memories of Sarah's dad and songs and tales from the war years still resided.

Her mother greeted her enthusiastically when she went on her weekly visit to the home. At first Sarah was fooled into thinking some miracle had happened and that her real mum had returned. 'I didn't know you were coming,' her mum said, her face twinkling with animation. She would smile at her neighbours slumped in identical blue, high-back chairs with wee-proof cushions as if she expected them to share her delight. Then Sarah realised her mother always said that but would say nothing more for the duration of the visit. She had not greeted Sarah by name for two years.

All the old ladies sitting in the lounge looked similar with their shrunken bodies and parchment faces topped and tailed by fluffy slippers and curly white hair. So similar that Sarah recently greeted the wrong person.

'Don't blame yourself. They all have the same hair style,' a care worker told Sarah. 'Not your fault. The hairdresser only does one style. She calls it "the queen".'

The hairdresser was more imaginative in other areas, though.

'Oh, she's lovely your mum, such a personality.'

Sarah wondered whether she was making it up or whether the threshold for having a personality was pretty low in there. She looked at her mother's neighbours: one old man muttered to himself and rhythmically raised a hand to his head where the skin was rendered raw by his compulsive scratching. An old woman on the right stared into the distance fiercely embracing an armful of stuffed animals. Probably. Or was her mum still manipulating her? Did she sense Sarah's resentment and was responding to it with silence – the only weapon she had left?

Sarah stroked the thin, pale skin of her mother's hand marbled with veins and brown liver spots, fragile as a bird's claw. One of the care assistants had painted her nails red but her mum had bitten off most of the polish and picked away at the rest. Sarah talked about her two daughters and tried to come up with amusing anecdotes. But when her mother occasionally stopped picking her nail polish and looked up, her washed out blue eyes continued to register bewilderment and another undefinable emotion. Sarah hoped this other emotion, if one could call it that, was not pain, but there was no way of knowing. It reminded Sarah of the look she saw in Rex's eyes when she took him to the vet's that one last time. It was a pleading 'I've had enough' sort of look. Or was Sarah merely projecting her own wishful thinking?

Sarah often got one of the wheelchairs from the cupboard near the care home office, dressed her mum in her outdoor coat and shoes, put a rug over her knees and pushed her into town. On this particular day she rummaged in her pockets for the spare pair of gloves she always carried for her mother, but she had forgotten them.

The wind was sharp. Billowing black clouds smothered the sky and needles of rain began to strike Sarah at an angle as they passed the churchyard. She put up her mother's hood and her own. Holding an umbrella was impossible with such powerful gusts and she needed both hands to push uphill. There would be no point giving one to her mum who had forgotten what it was for and would drop it. Sarah wondered if her mother would catch a cold which would turn into something fatal.

At a busy, traffic-clogged junction lorries spewed diesel as they screeched round the corner trying to beat the lights at the pedestrian crossing. Sarah put on the wheelchair's brake and watched for the green man symbol. There was always a long wait and, skin stinging, she tapped a tattoo on the black plastic. Staring down at the head huddled beneath the hood while huge black tyres thundered past a few centimetres away, she became aware of a familiar impulse. When they reached the high street she kept up a stream of chatter to bury the guilt.

'Oh, look, there's a sale on at M & Co. Do you want to go in here and look at the shoes? Shall I get you a magazine from Smith's? What do you fancy for lunch?'

She did not expect answers and did not get them. There was no body contact. They were just two marooned individuals connected by a wheelchair and genetics.

In summer it was easier. People looked happier and seemed more willing to make way for a wheelchair. Boxes full of gaudy summer bedding flanked the pavement and her mother – who had loved her garden - would notice them and point. Flowers had been a passion. Babies, too. Sarah would angle the chair so her mother could see any babies in the pub or the park. The babies didn't mind being stared at – they were used to it.

Occasionally there was other evidence of cognition. Six months ago her mother had asked a question when they were in Wetherspoons. 'Is the Post Office next door?' It was. When Sarah bought a watch battery, her mum became agitated and began rubbing her arm. Sarah, realising she missed her own, bought her a cheap one. As she fastened the watch round the thin wrist, the bleached out blue eyes looked up and she saw meaning behind them. 'Oh, you are good to me,' said her mum.

Sarah wanted to throw her arms around her mother, but pity had to be shut in a drawer along with the futility of hope. Her mum was once so full of fun and humour. Adored being the centre of attention. Loved other people. Leave her on a park bench for a few minutes and she would find a new friend and know their life story by the time Sarah returned. She was once the most important person in Sarah's life, the person whose good opinion she sought and valued above anyone's. Now her mother was reduced to a food-processing machine.

The carers said her mother still had a healthy appetite, and Sarah was grateful she no longer had to deal with the waste disposal. She remembered wrestling with her mum when she was still in her own home, trying to get her to use the commode when it was obvious she would not make it to the bathroom. Afterwards she realised why her mother had put up such a fight – she had hidden hundreds of pound notes in the commode. Thinking of food reminded Sarah that she had invited her daughter to supper that evening and had forgotten to take the meat from the freezer.

On Radio 4 that morning there was a debate about empathy fatigue, and Sarah wondered if it applied to her. She was a cognitive therapy counsellor, a professional listener, and people came to her with their problems. Kind and empathetic to her clients, she always kept tissues on her desk, but when it came to her mother, there seemed to be a void where her heart used to be. Week after week, while the fiction of her mother's existence was played out with ruthless monotony, Sarah feared that the sordid scenarios she created in her head had turned her into someone she despised. She hated the two-hour drive. She hated the care home with its smell of wee, over-boiled cabbage and disinfectant, peopled by the vacant eyes of the living dead, but most of all, she hated herself for hating it. Weary after the visits, she plotted and schemed.

She felt her mother would understand. Sarah based this on her mum's reaction to a friend brought back to life thanks to medical intervention, only to be left dribbling and incontinent with no feeling down one side.

'No resuscitation if that happens to me,' she had told Sarah and her sister. 'Promise me. I wouldn't want to live like that. On the receiving end of everyone's pity. Being a burden. No point.'

If her mum could express her rage about her helplessness and the theft of her independence and dignity. If she could take a swipe at the carers who wiped her bum like a baby and stuffed pads into her knickers, she would tell Sarah to go ahead. Wouldn't she?

Occasionally, a glimmer of the woman her mother had been would surface. This happened when a former nightclub singer and her guitar-playing husband performed at the home. They didn't just play war songs such as Vera Lynn's *We'll Meet Again* (which Sarah found ironic given most of the residents' mental absence) but The Beatles, Stones, Elton John and Rod Stewart. Her mum still knew all the words. Even the woman with the stuffed animals sat up straighter and joined in. The singer, overweight, bottle-blonde and big-bosomed, got right in their faces with her mike and flirted with them. Sarah would sing along with her mother, holding her hand, and was almost persuaded that the woman who had once loved her so fiercely still resided somewhere in that thin, wasted body. Was she still hanging on to life sustained by memories of her two daughters and their late father? But when the music stopped, the default state of bewilderment would reassert itself. Her mother would lower her head and resume picking at her nail polish. Sarah would grieve all over again for she had glimpsed her real mother. Just for a bit. And lost her all over again.

When the musicians came again just as the snowdrops began to poke their heads through the dark soil, Sarah once again held her mother's bony hand and began to sing. This time her mother did not join in but continued to pick her nail polish. The singer came up close but when her mother briefly raised her head she was frowning, her mouth agape. Sarah noticed that dribble had formed crusts at the corners of it. Her mother resumed her picking and the singer moved on. A boulder grew in Sarah's gut and on the way home she pulled into a layby, filled with the need to have a normal conversation with someone who cared. Fumbling for the mobile in her handbag she was dismayed to find the battery was flat.

Enough was enough. The following week when Sarah went to the home she got the wheelchair from the cupboard near the office. She dressed her mother in her outdoor coat and shoes, put a rug over her knees and pushed her towards town. When they stopped at the busy junction where lorries belching out diesel screeched round the bend, Sarah stopped at the kerb waiting for the lights to change. She stared at the wheelchair's brake. Her fingers twitched. If she flipped up the black plastic handle the wheels would roll. She scrunched up her eyes. Her hands tensed.

'Penny for them,' said a voice. 'Lights have changed, love.'

'Thanks,' she mumbled to the man who had tipped her off. She looked down. Felt light-headed.

'Oh, look, there's a sale on at M & Co,' she said. 'Do you want to go in here and look at the shoes? Shall I get you a magazine from Smith's? What do you fancy for lunch?'

She did not expect answers and did not get them.

Sarah planned to kill her mother next time she saw her. She was pretty sure she could get away with it. What worried her most was all the play-acting she'd have to engage in afterwards. Repressing the urge to confess. Lying to the kids.

The Prince-Frog

Hroubadour Tusk

Some kid at the Make-a-Wish foundation wanted to fight a Mummy. All the experts said it was too dangerous. They weren't prepared to risk the wrath of the undead. But Make-A-Wish were desperate. They had already rejected two of his wishes for being unfeasible, and really don't like saying no to three. At which point someone mentioned my name.

Fighting the Mummy didn't quite go to plan. These things rarely do. We had a job closing it back in its sarcophagus. Afterwards everyone congregated for a drink to sooth our nerves. The boy's parents even let him have one. Quite a day for the little lad.

I was the last to leave, staying long after the rest had said their goodnights, trying to flush the spectre of the shrieking Mummy from my head.

* * *

The next day, the Prince of Lilahpuhd approached me at breakfast. I'd seen him at the bar last night and remembered we'd spoken, though couldn't recall what it had been about.

"Mr. Tusk!"

He thrust a ticket into my hand. It transpired that last night I had agreed to join him on a cruise down the Nile. There was some issue he was desperate to discuss.

I wiped the memories of yesterday's nightmare from my eyes and followed him to where our boat was ready to depart. Maybe throwing myself into another job was exactly what was required.

* * *

The Prince took no notice of the bitter glares of our fellow passengers as the ticket inspector escorted us through to an area of the stern cordoned off for us to speak in private. We had the best view of the river but the Prince didn't seem to notice, absent-mindedly picking at the paint flaking away on the railing.

"Mr. Tusk, I have not always been a Prince. I was born a frog. One day I angered a frog-priestess, and she punished me by transforming me into a human prince. Lilahpuhd's not even a real place."

"No," I agreed, "I did think that was strange."

"Generations of frogs have come and gone and still I remain human. The priestess told me one way I could become a frog again, but," he sighed, "If you think getting a woman to kiss a frog is hard, getting a frog to kiss a man is nigh-on impossible."

He stared down into the river. "I can't go on any longer as a man. I must return to being a frog. I have heard, Mr. Tusk that you specialise in solving fantastical dilemmas such as mine?"

"I wouldn't say it's so much that I solve fantastical dilemmas," I corrected, "As that the solution tends to present itself while I'm around."

"Either shall do." He shook my hand. "Where do we start?"

Not having been born a frog myself, I'd never considered the possibility of needing to turn back into one. I tried to recall similar cases that might provide direction.

"Kissing a frog would have been my first move, but you say that's not worked. Have you tried asking a human magician to remove the curse?"

"Of course. They couldn't understand why I would want to."

"How about the original frog-priestess? The one who cursed you."

His head drooped even further towards the water.

"Dead. A nasty scuffle with an enchanted dragonfly."

I could see his desperation rising. He had come to me for an answer and all I could give him were solutions he'd already tried and found wanting. I pushed my brain harder, casting around me for inspiration.

"I assume you've tried doing a good deed?"

I stopped, seeing him shuffling his feet with embarrassment.

"You've done no good deeds?! Not even by accident?"

He turned red and mumbled, "Do you think it might help?"

"Who knows, but it's the first thing you should have tried! I wonder if you even really want to become a frog again."

"I do, I do!" He insisted. "So, what would count as a 'good deed'?"

Despite my sharp tone I was relieved. Things were looking far better than they had a moment ago. After the events of yesterday I was glad to have a more straightforward case. I focused on the task in hand.

"You're probably too late to play the 'making amends for past misdeeds' card," I began. "Maybe - "

My attention was grabbed by a Mummy climbing up the hull of the boat to stand, dripping wet, in front of us. The ticket inspector was nowhere to be seen.

It pointed its finger at us. Well, at me I suppose. The boat, and everyone on-board, started to melt.

I rushed the Mummy, trying to tip it overboard. But it was quicker than Boris Karloff would have you believe and sent me crashing into the railing. It shrieked at me and I felt my skeleton retreat. It was the same shriek that had been lodged in my brain after yesterday's battle. Then, I had taken it for a war cry. Now it seemed more like the Mummy was trying to tell me something. I tried to hear it, but no son of man had ears capable of hearing the Mummy's cry.

Oh, hang on.

I turned to the Prince, who was explicitly not a son of man. He was a son of frog. Sure enough, he didn't seem to be affected by the melting. He was just standing there watching. He saw my expression.

"What?"

"Can you understand it?" I hoped the words had come out clearly enough out of my melting jaw for him to understand.

"Yeah."

It was hard to express frustration while my eyebrows were sliding down into my nose, but I think I managed.

"Translate."

As he marched up to the Mummy I slid to the floor. I wanted to tell him to hurry, but I couldn't even croak out words any more. I heard him walk over to my side but couldn't turn my face to look at him.

"She says you woke her up and now she can't get back to sleep. She's afraid of the dark."

My back pocket, I tried to say. *Give her the torch in my back pocket.* It came out as a gargle. I felt the Prince leaning over me as I blacked out. The melting must have reached my skull.

* * *

When I came to, everything had returned to normal. The other passengers were their usual solid selves. The Mummy was sat on the railing, legs dangling over the side, looking slightly ashamed of herself. My torch was in her hands. I couldn't see the Prince. The clothes he had been wearing were in a pile on the deck, though his crown was missing. I went to speak to the Mummy.

"I just wanted to say, I am very sorry for disturbing you. I suppose I didn't think this one through. Please, keep the torch, and I promise to do better in future."

The Mummy stared at me while I demonstrated how to turn the torch on and off.

"Did you see where the Prince went?"

The Mummy pointed out to the river, before vanishing into smoke. I felt the warm glow of a job well done. I looked out, hoping for a glimpse of the Prince in his frog-form now his good deed had been performed. I wanted to say goodbye, and perhaps collect any reward he may have felt he owed me. But something wasn't right.

I don't know if you've ever seen a walrus wearing a crown. I hadn't. It was impossible to mistake for a frog as he looked at me mournfully.

"Your majesty?" I called, just to be sure. He nodded. His crown slipped off into the river.

He paddled after the boat. I threw him a fish that had beached itself next to me during the melting, praying that it hadn't once been the Sultan of Moldova or anything. The walrusprincefrog gobbled it up greedily.

"Well," I muttered, watching him eat, "It appears we still have a problem."

I Was Not Happy

Alan Davie

I was not happy when the doctor wouldn't give me pills for my headache.

I was not happy when the hospital said the tests showed that I needed surgery.

I was not happy when they put me to sleep.

I was not happy that I woke up and found I had to report my name and date of birth to a stern lady receptionist wearing white.

No I'm not at all happy, stuck here in this waiting room with a flock of old people.

Names are being called and gradually the room is emptying.

I have a fairly good idea of what is happening, but I expect I will learn more when I am summoned to the consulting room.

"Philip Edmondson to room 3."

Good, that must be me. I tap on the door and enter. An officious looking man in a white suit is seated behind a large desk.

"Philip Edmondson?"

I agree that this is my name.

"I have to tell you that you have passed over, you have lost your life on earth and you are now in the ante-rooms of heaven. (I had guessed correctly.) I need to inform you that I am obliged to review the file on your past life and will assess your future standing in paradise".

"We will go through your file together, to check its veracity. Let me firstly check your basic details. You are Philip John Edmondson? DOB 15/5/1962,.."

"Hey! Hold on, no, that's all rubbish. My name is Philip James Edmonson, there is no 'd' before son and my date of birth is 15th May 1952."

The large man looked a little confused. "But the file says... Ah, No, I'm sorry, it seems I have been given the wrong file"

He looked angry, scribbled a note and hit the plunger on the old-fashioned bell on his desk. Within seconds another white clad pretty lady entered from a side door.

"I have been given the wrong file. This is not good enough." He was angry. "I want this sorted out immediately. I also want a meeting with reception, the researchers and the compiler of this file immediately. This is completely unprofessional and unacceptable."

"I'll deal with it straight away," said the secretary and left.

I had the feeling that she had coped with her boss's anger before.

"Mr Edmonson, I do apologise for my staff's shortcomings, I assure you this is most unusual." He led me to the door. "Please return to the waiting room, I will call you again as soon as this is corrected."

I told him I was not happy.

All the previous occupants of the room had vanished. There was just a young girl sitting close to the entrance door. She had a child of about four clinging to her left leg.

"Excuse me, sir," she said. As I was the only other person in the room, I assumed she meant me. "Do you work here?"

I faced her, ready to explain why I was unhappy, but I saw her wide-eyed scared look and decided my problems were minimal. "Can I help you?" I said.

"I don't know where we are. I've got to get Roo to school, it's only her second week and she loves it so much. Why are we here? I...I don't understand." the words were rushing out of her and suddenly she raised her hands to her face and began to cry, the little girl at her side also began to sob.

I slipped into the chair next her. "It's alright," I said, "You are quite safe here." I have daughters of my own. I put my arm around her thin shoulders, and wondered if there were ridiculous PC rules here, too.

I didn't think it was up to me to explain that she was dead and had gone to heaven. So I fished in my pocket and found a couple of tissues which I handed to her. She wiped her eyes and blew her nose and surprisingly handed the wet tissues back.

"That's better; now, don't cry any more, it's going to be alright."

"Yes, Mummy, don't cry" piped the little girl."

"It's OK, Roo, Mummy is just being silly"

"Look," I said, "When they call your name, they will explain everything. All I can say is that you are in a better place than you have ever been in before. You see... you have crossed over and..."

"Sally Roberts and daughter to Room 4, please."

"Oh no, that's my name. What do I do? Where do I go?"

"It's alright. Come on I'll take you. Room 4 wasn't it?"

"OK, thanks. Come on Roo."

I escorted her to Room 4 and tapped on the door.

"Come in."

I was happy to hear a female voice. I turned the doorknob and pushed the door open. I was pleased to see a homely looking lady in flowing white advancing towards us.

"Sally? Come on in. And who is this lovely little princess?"

The door was closed firmly in my face, so I was unable to eavesdrop. I was not happy.

I returned to my seat in the now empty waiting room, thinking 'Poor little thing, she seemed so vulnerable, I hope she and the kid will be alright.'

Eventually my name was called again, this time everything was correct and I left the consulting room by the back door. I found myself in a charming sunlit garden. There were quite a few people here, talking in groups or strolling past the flower beds. It brought back childhood memories of seaside parks.

"Hey, Hi, Over here." I turned to see the girl beckoning to me.

"Hello, Sally, how are you?" I said. "Are you OK?"

"Oh yes. Isn't it great here? I love it. Hey you remembered my name... I don't even know yours."

"My name is Philip," I replied.

"Hello Phillip," she said rather formally shaking my hand. "I just wanted to thank you for looking after me, I was being silly. I understand what's happened now. They explained that Roo and I were hit by a lorry. What happened to you?"

"Botched hospital operation," I said. "Where is Roo?"

"She's over there, playing with the other kids." She pointed to where five or six children were running about, under the supervision of yet another lady in white.

"Tell me," I asked, "Her name, does it come from *Winnie the Pooh?*"

"Oh, that's one of her favourite DVDs. No its not, like, Kanga's baby Roo. Her real name is Ruby, you know like the song *Ruby, Ruby, Ruby, Ruubeeeh.*"

It didn't sound much like a song to me. "Ruby, that's a lovely name," I said, but thought, 'What a shame to shorten it.'

"They gave me a Grade D." Sally obviously liked to chatter.

"Me too," I said

"What?"

"They gave me a Grade D too."

"You must be kidding. You're Mr Nice Guy. I thought you would be a Grade A."

"No, I'm not that nice. I do have some sins in my past."

"That means we will probably go to the same...."

"Cloud," I suggested

When she realised I was joking she gave a light punch to my arm and started giggling.

"We might have to share a harp." Now she was laughing an infectious laugh. I started to laugh too.

"You have the wings today, I'll have them, tomorrow."

We were both laughing now, with no restraints. I saw people looking our way and smiling. It must have been a strange sight, an old bloke and a young girl sitting on a bench laughing together like old pals.

I felt good, in fact, I was happy.

A Shared Secret

Paul Walker

The dream crawls around the edges of my imagination as I knock on an open door and walk in. He's peering closely at his computer screen and tapping repeatedly with one finger on the keyboard. He doesn't look up, but gestures with his other hand at a chair by the side of his desk. He's younger than me and that's not a good start. I was hoping to unburden myself to someone older and wiser; an avuncular and understanding, grey-haired uncle wearing a tweed waistcoat with pocket watch, perhaps. This man, Dr Grundig, is new to the practice and has the appearance of a banker in faultless white shirt, pink tie and the bristled outline of a dark beard. His inattention is unnerving and adds a sourness to my discomfort.

His finger stops mid-poke and he moves his head towards me. 'Ah, yes, sorry Mr... Fisher. Please tell me why you're here today.' I don't know him, but something in his expression suggests that he recognises me.

'I'm having trouble sleeping, doctor.'

He's turned away to focus on his computer again. 'I see... it's been quite a while since we last saw you. Allergic reaction to a bee sting... eight years ago.' He turns to me with a look of triumph as though he's expecting me to congratulate him on the accuracy of his database. I shrug.

He clears his throat. 'Any idea what could be at the root of this problem? A relationship? Work? Moving house? A physical complaint?'

'It could be any number of things. I'm not sure...' My voice trails away to a faint murmur. I'm not ready to get to the nub of the matter, yet.

'OK, let's take a look at you.'

He asks me to take off my sweater and roll up my sleeve so that he can measure my blood pressure. The electronic device makes a mechanical, whirring sound as the strap tightens around my arm. He clicks his tongue when the whirring stops, then asks me to remove my shirt as he takes up his stethoscope. He listens to my chest – front and back – then takes a wooden spatula and looks inside my mouth. When he's finished, he returns to his computer and types at the keyboard for a few moments before he sits back in his chair and clasps his hands together.

'Your blood pressure is very high; much too high for a man of your age even allowing for "white coat" nervousness. Your chest is clear and you don't appear to have a throat infection.'

'I feel tired and I ache a little, but otherwise...' I don't know how to finish the sentence, so hunch my shoulders and offer a half-smile.

'There's normally a reason behind insomnia? Do you have an important appointment coming up?'

'A nightmare. I have a recurring nightmare. I'm even getting flashes of it now.'

'Tell me about it.'

'Well...' I swallow hard to try and dispel the bitter taste at the back of my mouth and place my hand on my right knee to stop it jigging. 'I'm driving a car along a street with parked cars either side.'

'Yes, please go on.' He's noticed the attempt to calm my leg.

'Something comes out between two cars and I hit it. It might be a dog, or...'

'Or what? A cat; a child?'

'I don't know. It might be a child. It's not clear. It happens too quickly. A bump, nothing more.'

'And then what happens?'

'I stop, I think, then drive on. The car is white. The street is empty, except for the parked cars.'

'Is that it?'

'Then the screaming starts. It's a mother's scream. It won't stop. It hurts...behind my eyes, in my chest...' Should I tell him more? The hospital bed; the incessant pinging of the life-support monitors; the smell of disinfectant; the small, limp body that I carry everywhere?

He looks thoughtful; troubled. He's trying to frame a question, then catches my eye and inclines his head inviting me to continue. I resist. The silence between us stretches too far. He breaks first.

'Mr Fisher, could this...'

'This is confidential, right? It's our secret?'

'Of course, this consultation is private, unless... Is there something else that you want to tell me?'

'It really happened.'

He unclasps his hands and sits forward in his chair. He clears his throat.

'Are you admitting to me that you may have injured or killed a child?'

'It's confusing. I may have done, but...' I've told him and I should feel a sense of release that this awful secret has passed to someone else, but he doesn't show any understanding or a willingness to absorb any of my pain and torment. '...I can't be certain.'

'When and where was the accident?'

'I'm not sure. It was near here and some time ago, I think. A week... a month? This nightmare has been with me for too long to remember when it started.' There's a noise in the corridor outside. Hushed voices. A feeling of panic grips my belly and I can smell my own fetid breath. I close my eyes tightly and shake my head. 'I had to let someone know. I can't keep this secret inside me any longer, but it's ours now. You won't divulge the content of this conversation to anyone else, will you?'

He ignores my question and asks another in return. 'How does your nightmare end, Mr Fisher?'

'I'm lying in a hospital bed, but I'm awake. A mother and child stand at the end of the bed, staring at me. The screaming has stopped, but their mouths are gaping; ugly, black and with jagged edges. I get out of bed and gather the child up in my arms. It has no weight. The mother turns her head away from me.'

'And then?'

'Then I come to see you, doctor.'

Flour White and Spindle Thin

Len Maynard

Dawn the colour of honey rose slowly over the verdant expanse of Flatland Marsh. Tom Henderson breathed in the crisp morning air, pulled a packet of cigarettes from his pocket and lit one, sucking in the tobacco smoke and rolling it around his mouth before drawing it deeply into his lungs. His first morning in his new job of marsh-warden and already he was grateful for his redundancy from the electronics company. The redundancy had given him an opportunity to reassess his life. With his wife Louise making enough money from illustrating to cover most of their needs, his role as breadwinner had become more and more superfluous. It was time for a complete break, and he'd grabbed this chance to escape the rat race with both hands. Now he was glad he had done so.

He surveyed the landscape, taking in the rough tussocks of scrubby grass and the torpid pools of water that harboured all manner of wildlife. To the west were outcrops of granite, dark soldiers standing guard over the marsh; to the east the town of Risley. And beyond the marsh, the cold grey waters of the North Sea, separated from the land by mud flats.

He ground the cigarette under the thick rubber sole of his boot and headed back. The house that came with the job was nothing grand, nothing more than a two bedroomed cottage sitting in half an acre of land. There was a garden, an orchard and a large ornamental pond, but the garden was unkempt and running to weed, the orchard nothing more than a handful of diseased apple trees, with a couple of pears to give variety. The pond was choked with weed and harboured nothing but frogs and newts, the fish having long died off. His predecessor obviously had no time for maintenance, either that or couldn't be bothered, and the decor in the house mirrored the sad state of the garden with peeling wallpaper, chipped and browning paintwork, and the dishevelled feel of an old man long since past his prime.

Louise saw the place as a challenge and had set about stripping walls and repainting doorways with all the passion of a zealot. She'd always supported him, always been there to bolster his confidence and to embrace his sometimes hare-brained schemes, and he loved her for it.

As he came upon the house through the orchard, he picked up a windfall apple from the ground beneath one of the stunted trees, rubbed it on his jacket until the skin shone, then bit into it, spitting the flesh out quickly as sour juice filled his mouth. He tossed the apple away with a grimace. Perhaps he could use them to make cider. As he passed the large weather-beaten shed that occupied space to the right of the pond he noticed the door was slightly ajar. He could see the padlock that once secured it lying on the grass, the hasp hanging loose from the door.

Inside the shed everything seemed much as it had the day before when he'd been looking for some shears. Nothing appeared to have been stolen, but there was something different about the place. In the corner a muddy tarpaulin was wrapped around a sleeping form.

He approached silently, just getting a glimpse of a head poking out from under the tarpaulin. The sleeping figure was a young boy, who looked no more than twelve years old, with pale skin and a shock of white-blond hair. The tarpaulin rose and fell gently with the boy's breathing but other than that there was no movement; the boy was as still as a statue.

A sudden gust of wind caught the door and slammed it into its frame, making Tom jump. He spun around at the noise, caught a small tower of terracotta pots on the shelf with his arm and sent them crashing to the floor. When he looked back the boy was awake and on his feet staring at him wildly.

He was tall for his age, almost as tall as Tom, and was dressed in clothes that were nothing more than rags. His feet were bare, scratched and muddy, the toenails filthy and unclipped. The pale hair flopped over a face as white as flour, and the boy's limbs were spindle thin, looking as if they might snap at the slightest touch. Obviously malnourished and uncared for the boy presented a sorry sight. He regarded Tom with frightened eyes, looking past him at the door and his means of escape.

'It's all right,' Tom said. 'I won't hurt you.'

The boy, still badly frightened, cocked his head to one side at the sound of Tom's voice, puzzlement jostling with fear in his eyes, almost as if he'd never heard a human voice before and was trying to ascertain what the strange sound was.

Tom tried again. 'What's your name?' he said and took a step towards him.

The boy bared a row of brilliantly white teeth and growled deep in his throat, and then, with a movement so quick it took Tom completely by surprise, the boy darted past him. Tom reached out and caught his arm, his fingers encircling thin flesh and bone. The boy ducked his head and bit Tom's exposed wrist, the teeth cutting through the soft skin. Tom imagined them grinding against his bones. He cried out and swore, pulling his arm away and clutching it to his chest.

The boy crashed through the door, sending it careening back against the shed wall. Tom screwed his eyes tight with the pain from his wrist and tried to follow, but his foot rolled over one of the fallen pots and he stumbled, falling down, one knee taking his full weight and sending fresh paroxysms of pain lancing through his body.

By the time he got to his feet and stumbled outside, the boy was nothing but a pale shape disappearing through the trees towards the marsh. Tom rubbed at his bruised knee and limped back to the house.

* * *

'You should go to Casualty,' Louise said as she swabbed disinfectant into the bite. The teeth marks were red and angry, the skin around each puncture puckered and swollen. 'Human bites are more poisonous and bacteria-filled than most other animals.'

'Thanks. You're making me feel better by the minute. Just disinfect it and wrap a bandage round it. It'll be fine.'

'I wonder where he came from,' she said pressing a gauze pad over the wound. 'I know there's an orphanage over Hepton way. Perhaps he came from there.'

Tom shook his head. 'No, I don't think so. I told you he was dressed in rags. He's been living rough for some time.'

'Perhaps we should notify the police.'

'And face all those questions? No, there's probably a family of travellers in the area – gypsies. He was probably on a foraging mission and decided to bed down here for the night rather than try to find his way back in the dark.' It was an unlikely scenario and Tom knew it, but he wanted a quick answer to the problem of the boy. He wanted nothing to interfere with the peace and quiet of his newly discovered idyllic lifestyle.

Louise tore off two strips of sticking plaster and taped them over the bandage to secure it. 'I still think you should get it looked at.'

He grinned reassuringly. 'I'll live; besides, I've got loads to do. There's the fence to repair.'

'That's not going to take you all day,' she said.

He reached up and stroked her neck fondly. 'No it won't, but I can think of better ways of spending the afternoon than sitting in A and E, can't you?'

His finger tickled the base of her hairline and she felt warmth spread through her body. She shuddered slightly and kissed the top of his head. 'I've got to work too, you know?' she said, but the thought of spending the afternoon curled up in bed together was a strong temptation. 'You'd better get on then,' she said, returning his grin.

* * *

The fence was on the west side of the marsh where the boggy ground bordered a field that once belonged to a neighbouring farm. The farm suffered badly in the last foot and mouth outbreak, the farmer losing all his stock. After seeing his livelihood and indeed his complete way of life decimated by the disease and the draconian prevention methods of the Ministry of Agriculture, the farmer took a shotgun to his wife and children, and finally himself. It was a tragic, but not a unique case. Tom could only guess at the despair the man felt.

In the time the farm had stood empty nature stepped in and started to reclaim the land that was once grazing for the herd of Friesians, and the field now resembled a meadow with poppies, campion and other wild flowers vying for space with the long grass that waved softly in the morning breeze.

Tom crouched down in front of the first post and hammered a heavy staple into the wood, thread the end of a coil of wire through the eye and twisted it around itself. Then he hammered the staple flush, securing the wire, picked up the coil and carried to the next post, letting the wire trail out behind him.

Repairing the fence was necessary. The field was now a popular place for local children. Games of cowboys and Indians and cops and robbers could easily end in tragedy should one of the participants stray too far into the greedy marsh.

He crouched down at the next post, held the wire up and surrounded it with a staple, and then using a length of wood twisted into the wire to serve as a lever he stretched it until it was as taut as a guitar string and hammered the staple home. He plucked the wire, listening to the deep, tense note it produced with satisfaction.

He was about to move on to the next post when he stopped and looked around. It was a familiar tingle down his spine: a sensation he always got when he felt he was being watched. For a moment he thought Louise had come out to join him on the marsh, but he looked back towards the house and there was no sign of her. He pushed himself upright and turned three hundred and sixty degrees, his eyes scanning the land in all directions, but there was nobody to see. The marsh and surrounding areas were deserted, with not even a rabbit or deer to be seen.

He scratched his head and moved on to the next post. It was unusual for his instincts to play him false, but for the next two hours as he worked, he'd stop and stand every so often, convinced he could feel another's eyes upon him.

* * *

Louise propped herself up on her elbow and looked at her sleeping husband. The lines that had been etched into his face by strain and worry were smoothing out, the dark circles under his eyes gradually fading. It was everything to do with the new job and moving here. It was as though ten years had been wiped from his features. He slept now with a peaceful, almost beatific look on his face. She smiled at him fondly and swung her legs to the floor, careful not to wake him, and went to shower.

His renewed interest in sex was also a sign the new position was having a restorative effect. At thirty-five she was beginning to feel that this aspect of her life was in suspended animation. His lack of enthusiasm for the physical side of their relationship almost caused her to look elsewhere. Almost, but not quite. She'd had the opportunity – an opportunity almost too tempting to resist, but was now grateful she hadn't succumbed to the temptation. She loved Tom with a passion undimmed in the years since they'd got together at university, and now that carefree, sexy man was finally returning to her.

She had few regrets in their marriage. The absence of children was one but, as she grew older, even that was beginning to fade. The miscarriages were now ancient history and she was beginning to accept the doctor's prognosis that she would never be able to have children. It was painful at first, devastatingly painful, and difficult to deal with, and the strain it put on the marriage was intense, but gradually the pain eased, and the hormonal thrust that fuelled her desire to reproduce gradually dimmed, like a guttering candle using up the last of the oxygen in a sealed jar.

Besides, she had nieces and nephews now, and her friends had children. There was plenty of opportunity to indulge the maternal side of her nature, if only by proxy – at least that's what she told herself.

She went downstairs and made coffee, pouring herself a cup and taking it back to the spare bedroom they'd already converted into a studio for her. Taped to the drawing board was a pencil sketch she'd been working on while Tom was outside fixing the fence. She picked up a pencil and shaded a couple of areas, then went across to the window and picked up the binoculars, lying on the sill where she'd left them. She put them to her eyes and scanned the area where the granite outcrops jutted rudely up from the surrounding countryside.

He was no longer there, the subject of her picture – the painfully thin boy with white hair who'd sat cross-legged on top of one of the monoliths, watching Tom as he worked. It didn't matter he was no longer there. She'd captured his likeness perfectly, and when Tom awoke she'd show him the picture and ask him if this was the lad he'd encountered in the shed.

She took a sip of coffee and went back to the drawing board. Staring hard at the boy's face, wondering what elements of life could bring such a look of sadness to one so young.

'It looks just like him.'

She hadn't heard Tom come up behind her, but he was there, his arms around her waist, nuzzling her neck and staring over her shoulder at the sketch. He took her coffee cup from her and filled his mouth. She nudged him in the ribs with her elbow. 'Get your own,' she said.

'So this is what you get up to while you're supposed to be working,' he said, peering out through the window at the granite monolith. 'So that's why I kept getting the feeling I was being watched. How long was he there?'

'Long enough for me to do this. He sat there as still as a statue and watched you while you worked. An hour, maybe more.'

'You should have come and told me.'

'And have you haring after him. He was too good a subject to miss. I can use this image in the fairy book I'm doing next. Don't you think he looks a bit fairy-like?'

'Nah, the ears aren't pointed enough. Looks bloody weird though... as if he hasn't been out in the sun for years. Flour white and spindle thin. That's the phrase that repeats itself in my mind whenever I think about him.'

'It's a great title for the picture,' Louise said. 'I'll suggest it. You never know, Marion might write a story about him.' Marion Wheeler was a writer of children's books. Louise had illustrated every one to see print and they'd developed a mutually beneficial working relationship. They trusted each other, and that was important.

He kissed her neck again. 'Come back to bed.'

'You're insatiable. No. I've wasted enough time today. Go back out onto the marsh and do what marsh-wardens are supposed to do.'

'Spoilsport,' he said and gave her a final squeeze before going back to the bedroom to dress.

When she was alone Louise went back to the window and picked up the binoculars again, raking the countryside with the high magnification lenses, hoping to see a flash of white hair, a glimpse of pale skin. Something to reassure herself that he was still out there. Somehow it was important to her, but she hadn't yet begun to fathom out why.

* * *

The evening was spent in front of the television. She'd finished work about six, in time to prepare a lasagne for their dinner, and they'd eaten it off trays on their laps, watching the unlikely scenarios being played out on a popular soap opera.

He put down his knife and fork and set the tray at his feet. 'What's wrong?' he said.

'Wrong? Nothing's wrong. Why?'

'You seem to be in another place. For the past half hour you've been glancing up at the window as if you're expecting to see something there.'

She smiled ruefully. It was true, but she hadn't realised she was being that obvious. 'It's the boy. I can't seem to get him out of my mind. What if he's still out there? It's a filthy night.' Late that afternoon black storm clouds rolled in from the sea. They'd done nothing for an hour or so, except to growl menacingly, as if showing their displeasure. Then the first flash of lightning fizzed across the sky and the heavens unleashed a downpour causing Tom to take shelter under a nearby hornbeam. Not a sensible move in an electrical storm, but he figured the hornbeam was lower than the surrounding trees and was unlikely to be struck, and its dense crown afforded at least some protection from the torrent hammering down from the sky.

'Well if he is still out there, which I doubt, I dare say he's got enough savvy to find some shelter.'

'Did you leave the shed open?'

'No. I fixed the hasp and padlocked it again. It's a shed not a doss house.'

'But...' she started to protest, but left the rest unsaid. She didn't want to make an issue of it. She didn't really want to let Tom know just how much the pale boy had come to dominate her thoughts over the last few hours. 'As you say, he's probably used to being outdoors. I like my comfort too much to begin to contemplate what it must be like to sleep under the stars. That's why I never joined the girl guides.'

'I'll keep a look out for him tomorrow... and if he shows himself again and you see him, come and tell me.'

'Yes,' she said thoughtfully, gathering up the trays and taking them through to the kitchen. 'Yes I'll do that.'

* * *

But the boy didn't appear the next day, or that day after that. On the Saturday morning they drove into Risley to shop. The larder was alarmingly depleted, and they had virtually cleared the stocks in the freezer. Laden with bags from the supermarket they returned to the car park where they'd left Tom's Land Rover to find the window on the passenger side smashed. A pool of small glass cubes littered the floor and seat.

'How can they get away with this in broad daylight?' Tom said angrily. 'I thought this car park was patrolled.'

Louise was looking in through the broken window. 'But what were they after? There was nothing in here to tempt them except the CD player, and they haven't touched it.'

'Perhaps they were disturbed before they had a chance to grab it.'

Louise ran her hand through her short dark hair. 'My jacket's gone.'

'Jacket?'

'The Barbour I keep on the back seat... in case the weather turns. It's gone.'

'I can't see there'd be much resale value in a waxed jacket, can you?' Tom said, his mind still weighing up the cost of a replacement window. 'You're sure it's not hanging up at home?'

'Definitely. I wore it last week when we went to that furniture auction. Don't you remember? By the time we got there the weather had brightened up. I distinctly remember taking it off and slinging it onto the back seat. I didn't put it back on, and I certainly never took it back to the house.'

Tom was using a piece of cardboard torn from one of their boxes to scrape the glass from the seat. 'I'll tidy it up more thoroughly when we get back. This'll do for now. I still can't believe that someone would break in to a car just to steal a jacket.'

'They might if they were cold...' she said. Or if the only clothes they possessed were rags, she thought, but kept the thought to herself. It came unbidden into her mind and she tried to turn it away, but it remained, niggling at her during the blustery journey home. The image of the pale boy, huddled under a tree somewhere, hugging her waxed jacket tightly around him to stave off the elements was strangely comforting. At least I'm doing something, she thought, then immediately chided herself for being so ridiculous. The chances of the pale boy being the one who'd broken into the Land Rover were remote. More likely it was a local tearaway, disturbed, as Tom speculated, before he had a chance to get away with anything more valuable. Perhaps he thought the coat would contain some money, or even a packet of cigarettes – muggings had taken place for less. As they pulled into the drive she shook the thoughts away and tried to concentrate on the meal she was going to cook for them both tonight.

* * *

Tom stood at the sink in the bathroom and slid the nail scissors under the edge of the bandage. The wound was throbbing and itching like mad. He guessed it was probably infected, but said nothing to Louise, fearing a reprimand for not going to the hospital as she suggested. He snipped at the bandage, careful not to nick his skin, wincing as he saw the angry pus-filled bite mark.

He touched it gingerly with his finger and winced again as a hot pain shot up his arm. 'Damn it!' he said under his breath and reached into the medicine cabinet on the wall for some antiseptic. The pale yellow liquid made contact with the wound and for a moment he thought he would pass out. It was like, pouring acid onto raw flesh. He gripped the edge of the sink, waiting for the searing pain to ease, beads of sweat popping out like tiny moonstones on his forehead.

Gradually the pain abated and he took a deep breath, mopping the perspiration from his brow with a towel. Louise kept the bandages in a small first aid box under the sink. He took out a fresh bandage and tore off the wrapper, then put his hand flat against the wall and started to twist the dressing around his wrist. He figured he'd be able to manage without Louise's attention, but fumbled once and the bandage dropped to the floor, spilling out like a party streamer. He swore, gathered it up and started the laborious process again.

He'd been concentrating on wrapping the wound, and it was only when he'd finished and was reaching for a strip of sticking plaster that he noticed the hand itself.

The skin from his wrist down was almost bleached of colour, pale and dead looking. He held both hands out under the light above the vanity unit. His other hand looked normal, pink and healthy, making the other one look significantly worse in comparison. He flexed the fingers of the pale hand. Was it his imagination, or was there a slight numbness there? His fingers moved when he wanted them to move, but the movements seemed sluggish, uncoordinated.

'What are you doing in there?' Louise called from outside the door.

'Won't be a moment,' he called back and hurriedly stuck the plaster over the edge of the bandage, rolling down the sleeve of his shirt to hide it. 'Sorry,' he said, opening the door. 'Didn't know you were waiting.'

'You're flushed,' she said, almost an accusation.

'Am I? Must be the central heating. I'll check the thermostat.'

Her eyes narrowed and she shook her head. 'Feels fine to me,' she said, and pushed past him into the bathroom. He heard the lock click and went to pour himself a stiff drink.

The pale hand held the drink and it shook slightly as he raised the glass to his lips. The whisky burnt his throat and he gave an involuntary shudder as the liquid reached his stomach. He wasn't a drinker these days, though it had been different several years ago when he was getting through three or four bottles of whisky a week. But those were troubled times. Hospitalisation and countless tests for Louise, and the endless recriminations and tears that had threatened to burst their marriage asunder.

The taste of the scotch on his tongue brought the memories of that time flooding back. He screwed the cap back on the bottle and put it back in the cupboard, then went through to the kitchen and rinsed out the glass. Then he switched the coffee machine on, brewing up a strong espresso to remove the taste of alcohol from his mouth. He had no wish to revisit those times. They were bleak and depressing years. The tedious monthly ritual of taking temperatures, judging the ovulation cycle, and the mechanical, passionless sex. Baby making. Relentless and unsuccessful baby making. He heard Louise moving about upstairs and glanced down at his hand. She'd notice before much longer and she'd recommend a trip to the hospital, or the doctor's at least. And he couldn't really tell her of his aversion to anything medical, couldn't begin to explain the emotions visiting such places stirred in him.

The books she'd read focused on the women, their bodies, their emotions; how they could cope with the loss of a child, of the endless, unpitying struggle to conceive. The male partner was seen very much as a necessary adjunct to that struggle. A seed supplier, nothing more. How could he tell her that his drive to reproduce was almost as strong as hers? He was an only child, the last of his line. The family name stopped with him, and while her hormones and that indefinable thing called maternal instinct drove her, his need was more pragmatic. He didn't want to be the last, the end of the chapter. He wanted his genes perpetuated. He wanted the immortality a child would have provided. The crushing monthly disappointment when her period started affected him just a deeply as it did her. And while she cried and he held her, being strong for her, so his mind screamed in despair. The drink silenced the scream and deadened the pain. And it had also nearly destroyed him.

He took another sip of coffee and swilled it around his mouth, getting rid of the final lingering taste of scotch. Why he should be dredging up those memories again he wasn't sure. He hadn't thought about them for years. But now they were back pushing their way to the forefront of his mind, and he wondered what had triggered them.

* * *

Louise didn't see the pale boy again for a number of days, though she continued to pick up the binoculars on occasion and search the marsh and beyond, hoping to catch sight of him. The following Thursday Tom took the Land Rover into town to get the window fixed. He'd repaired it temporarily with a sheet of thick polythene, but that was only a stopgap, and as autumn gradually eased its way towards winter, he couldn't delay the inevitable. The Land Rover window would take a hefty chunk out of their monthly budget, and these days they had to be careful with their money. The marsh warden's job paid a good deal less than his previous position, and Louise's income was, by its nature, sporadic but the vehicle was not only necessary in his job, it was also their lifeline, their means of getting to town to bring supplies back to the isolated cottage. It had to be attended to.

She watched him go, waving from the gate, until he turned the corner at the end of the lane, then she went back to the house. In her study she taped a fresh piece of paper to the drawing board and sat for a moment waiting for inspiration to strike. She picked up her pencil and made a few exploratory lines on the page but her mind remained exasperatingly barren.

Pushing herself away from the board in frustration she went across to the filing cabinet in the corner to rummage through the folders of photographs and clippings from magazines – her source material. But she could find nothing to inspire her. She couldn't remember the last time she was blocked like this. Usually the muse that sat on her shoulder rose to the challenge of virgin paper and fed her something with which to fill it. But the muse today was obstinately silent. Perhaps she was asleep.

Louise slid the drawer back into the cabinet and crossed to the window. She reached for the binoculars and stopped.

The pale boy was standing in the back garden, staring up at the window. She smiled slightly when she saw he was wearing her waxed jacket. Her instincts had been right.

She hurried from the room and down the stairs, hoping the boy would still be there when she reached the garden.

He was.

He took a step backwards as she opened the back door and stepped outside, but other than that he didn't seem alarmed by her appearance.

She stood still, facing him. She'd never seen anybody with skin so white and hair so fair. Almost albino, but the eyes were dark – deep black pools that regarded her with something like wry amusement.

'Hello,' she said softly, worried that if she raised her voice much above a whisper the boy might take flight.

He said nothing but continued to stare for a moment then made a quick beckoning motion with his hand, turned and walked slowly to the gate that led onto the marsh. At the gate he stopped, turned to look at her and beckoned again.

'I can't go with you,' she said. 'I've work to do,' she added unconvincingly.

He didn't move.

'Let me get my coat and lock the house,' she said, curiosity beating her reservations into submission.

When she returned to the garden he hadn't moved, but as she drew close he turned and strode out into the marsh.

He moved with a curious grace, like a pale deer, sure-footed, without effort, picking his way between the muddy pools and hopping from tussock to tussock with the confidence that comes from long familiarity.

Louise followed as best she could, trying to keep in his footsteps, trying hard to avoid the lethal, murky pools that threatened to suck the shoes from her feet, to grab her legs and draw her down into the mire.

A mist had blown in from the sea, and the further she got into the marsh the thicker the mist became. Occasionally she lost sight of him altogether and she had to call out, to urge him to wait for her. He'd appear out of the mist, a small smile playing on his lips, and wait for her to, almost but not quite, catch up to him.

I must be mad, she thought as she picked her way through the morass. Tom would be furious if he knew what she was doing. But Tom would be away all morning, and probably much of the afternoon. Once the window of the Land Rover was fixed he intended to go and see his employer at the local council office to discuss plans for a picnic area the council, in their wisdom, decided would draw sight-seers to the area.

'To their death, more like,' Tom grumbled when he told her about the plan.

She stopped and looked back towards the house, but the mist had closed in behind her like thick gauze curtains, hiding the house from her. She had no choice now. She had to follow the boy. She'd never find her way back home, and the thought of wandering around in the lethal marsh made her baulk.

Ahead of her, out of the mist, appeared a small wooden built hut. It was ramshackle, its palings worn and rotted, the roofing felt split and curling over the front of the hut. There were no windows but a narrow horizontal slit at its front gave away its purpose. It was a bird-watcher's hide. A place for avian enthusiasts to decamp and mount their cameras and binoculars in the hope of catching a glimpse of the rare and endangered birds that made the marsh their home.

The boy was standing in front of the hide, his arms hanging loosely at his sides, waiting for her. When she was within six feet of him he ducked around the side of the hut and disappeared.

She jumped over a small boggy pool, stumbled and reached out to the wall of the hut to steady herself. The rough wood split under her touch and tiny splinters embedded themselves in her hand. She sucked in her breath and swore, and then, finding the ground firm under her feet, moved round in the direction the boy had taken.

There was no sign of him. It was as if the mist had swallowed him.

She called out and strained to hear a reply, but the air was silent, oppressively silent, as if a blanket had been thrown over the world, killing all sound. She reached the door of the hut and pushed it open, but it was empty; the only sign of human habitation being a discarded crisp packet and several empty soft drink cans.

She fought down a swell of panic and stepped outside. She called again, and this time there was a response.

The mist in front of her parted and a small girl stepped out. She was five or six, her hair as white as the boy's and her limbs as thin, if not thinner than his. She looked emaciated and Louise felt a surge of pity. 'Oh, you poor thing,' she said, crouching down to the girl's level, trying to reassure her with her body language that she presented no threat to her.

The child stood, unmoving, watching her with a mildly curious expression. Like the boy she was dressed in rags, the material threadbare and filthy, torn in places, allowing Louise to catch glimpses of the unnaturally pale flesh beneath.

The girl wound a strand of white hair around her thumb and pushed the whole lot into her mouth.

'I won't hurt you,' Louise said, and held out her arms. She just wanted to hug the child, to reassure her, and to carry her back home. She needed to report this to the proper authorities. For a child of this age to be allowed to get in this state was nothing short of criminal. If the parents were around here, she would have no compunction in telling them exactly what she thought of their parenting skills.

The little girl moved forward so gracefully it was almost as if she was gliding over the muddy grass. To her horror Louise noticed the little girl's feet were bare, wet mud squelching up between her toes.

When she was within reach Louise closed her arms around her in a tight embrace and stood upright, lifting the girl off her feet. She was feather-light, insubstantial like the mist that surrounded them. The girl wrapped her arms around Louise's neck, pulling herself in closer, as if craving the warmth of Louise's body. She buried her face into the protective shoulder, nuzzling close against Louise's breast.

The bite, when it came, was so shocking and so painful, that for a moment Louise just stood there, feeling the pain, and the tickling motion of a tiny tongue flicking over the wound.

With a cry she pushed the child away from her, holding her at arm's length, staring questioningly into the watery blue eyes. The expression on the little girl's face was serene as she licked her blood-specked lips. There was no malice there, no malevolence.

And suddenly Louise understood why she'd been brought here. With tears streaming down her face she hugged the child close to her again and let her feed.

* * *

Tom arrived home at about two, slamming the door behind him and walked into the lounge, a string of expletives issuing from his mouth. The meeting with the council had not gone well. Their decision to site the picnic area on the edge of one of the most treacherous stretches of marsh was, in his opinion, sheer folly, but his protests were met with bland bureaucratic platitudes. 'After all, Mr Henderson, you are only warden on the marsh. Should anything happen, which we sincerely doubt will, you would not be held responsible. And we must look at the broader picture. The shops and cafés in the area that would undoubtedly benefit from an influx of fresh revenue.'

He gave up at that point. He knew that financial kickbacks and promises of favours had already been made, and that the decision had already been taken.

Louise listened to his tirade of several minutes before saying, 'Why don't you sit down, calm down, and I'll make us a cup of tea?'

He flopped into an armchair with a sigh. She was right, as usual, he'd taken this job to escape stress, not to immerse himself again in battles he'd no hope of winning. 'How's your day been?' he called.

'Interesting,' she called back from the kitchen. She was wearing a high rolled-neck sweater to hide the bite marks on her chest and neck, but the chenille was irritating the wounds, making them itch. 'I'll tell you about it later,' she added.

He sank back in the chair and closed his eyes, letting the tension ebb from his body.

'You're going grey,' she said. She was standing behind him holding two steaming mugs of tea.

He glanced up at her. 'Is it any wonder, after the day I've had?' He held her eyes for a moment. 'You're being serious, aren't you?'

She nodded. 'I'd never noticed before, but there are definitely a few silver ones threading their way through now.'

'Shit!' he said and pushed himself to his feet, crossing to the mirror and pulling his hair this way and that. She was right. And it was more than just a couple of stray premature greys. Silver strands made up about a quarter of the brown untidy thatch that covered his head. He was sure they hadn't been there this morning when he'd been drying his hair after the shower, but then he hadn't been looking for them.

'But I'm only thirty-five. It's a bit young for all this.'

'I think it's dead sexy,' she said, coming up behind him and wrapping her arms around his waist. 'After you've had your tea, do you fancy coming for a walk?'

'A walk? Where?

'On the marsh. I made an interesting discovery today. I'd like to show you.'

He shrugged. 'Fine.' Then he thought for a moment. 'You haven't been walking around out there on your own, have you? I did warn you...'

'It's all right. I had company. Finish your tea. I'll tell you as we walk.'

* * *

An east wind had kicked up and blown the mist back out to sea. As they picked their way through the marsh Tom checked his watch. 'This'd better not take long. We've only got two hours of daylight at the most. We'll never find our way back in the dark, and I really don't fancy calling the rescue services to come and find us.' He patted his jacket pocket, feeling the reassuring bulge of his mobile phone. He'd brought it along as a precaution, but he hoped he wouldn't have to use it.

'Not far now. I wasn't sure I'd be able to find it on my own, but it all seems so familiar now.'

He slipped from a tussock of grass and buried his boot in the mud to the ankle. He swore savagely and yanked it free, groaning as water seeped over the top of the leather and soaked his sock. 'You still haven't explained what we're doing here.'

She glanced back at him, an annoyingly enigmatic smile on her face. 'No, I didn't, did I? Wait and see.'

'Bugger that!' he said and stopped walking. 'You either explain or I'm going back.'

She looked at him steadily, trying to decide whether or not he was bluffing. There was steel in his eyes and his chin jutted forwards pugnaciously. She decided not to call his bluff. 'It was the boy,' she said simply. 'He came to the house earlier... He was wearing my Barbour.' she added, a fond smile spreading over her lips.

'So he *was* the lout who smashed my window. When you see him again you might like to get the money out of him to pay for it.'

'That doesn't matter now,' she said. The wind was cold and cut through the thin material of her jacket, but she didn't feel cold. A mixture of excitement and adrenaline was warming her from within. 'It's all so perfectly clear to me now.'

'What is?'

'The reason we're here. The real reason you took the job.'

He sighed. 'I took the job because it was the only thing I could find that would take me completely out of the rat race. And that's the reason... the real reason.'

'But we were guided. Call it providence, fate, whatever you like, but you were destined to find and take that job, and we were destined to come to this place together. Come on,' she said, starting to walk again. 'Just a little bit further.'

He shook his head but followed.

'And don't think I haven't noticed your hand,' she said as she walked. 'I know you've been trying to hide it from me. But that's all part of it, don't you see?'

He flexed the fingers of the hand that was completely numb now and almost bleached white.

'And your hair. Can't you see what's happening to us?'

'All I can see is that you're leading us on some wild goose chase, and that you're starting to sound deranged.'

She laughed. 'O ye of little faith,' she said. 'Look, just up ahead.'

The hide was a few hundred yards ahead of them.

'That old place,' he said incredulously. 'But it's derelict. I checked it out a few days ago. You haven't seriously brought me out here to see...'

She hushed him. 'Keep your voice down. You'll scare her.'

'Scare who?' he said, but she was starting to run now and the wind whipped the words from his lips and carried them across the marsh and out to sea. He was sure she hadn't heard him.

They reached the hide together, Tom having to sprint to catch up with her. She held out her arm to stop him going any further. 'Quiet now,' she said, putting her finger to her lips.

He said nothing, alarmed at her behaviour, but curious to see how this was going to resolve itself. He felt a wetness in his palm and looked down. The bandage on his wrist was crimson where the wound had opened and started to bleed again. He brought his wrist up and hugged it to his chest, but there was no pain, just a curious pulling sensation, as if unseen hands were plucking at the bandage.

Louise was calling softly. 'It's me. I've come back, just like I said I would. Are you there?'

For a moment there was absolute stillness and absolute silence. Then came the sound of a footfall from behind a stand of trees. Louise reached back and gripped his arm excitedly. 'She's here.' Then she slipped off her jacket and pulled off her sweater.

He saw the bite marks for the first time. 'Louise!' he said, but a movement in front of them distracted his attention as a small, filthy girl stepped out from behind the shelter of the trees. She was dressed in rags and her white hair hung in rat's tails. Louise sank to her knees and held out her arms. The girl ran forward, casting furtive glances at Tom who stood, open-mouthed, hardly daring to believe what he was seeing.

The girl fell into Louise's embrace, buried her face into Louise's neck, tongue reaching for the raw flesh.

With a cry Tom lashed out with his foot, catching the girl in the chest and knocking her out of his wife's arms. The girl landed on her back on the spongy ground and with a guttural snarl rolled over onto her hands and knees, poised, ready to leap at him.

He grabbed Louise roughly by the arm and hauled her to her feet. 'Run!' he said, striding out onto the marsh. 'Run now!'

She was resisting him, sobbing. 'Tom, No!'

He took no notice. All he wanted to do was to get them as far away from this place as possible. He was dragging her along behind him, oblivious to her protests, yanking her impatiently if she stumbled. 'It's why we're, here,' she cried. 'Don't you see?'

He glanced back at her and stopped dead. The colour had drained from her hair, leaving it a stark white. And even as he watched the pounds seemed to be falling away from her body. He watched transfixed as her skin bleached and grew translucent. He let go of her arm, as if it were something alien. She stood erect, tossing back her pale hair. 'Don't you see?'

He felt a sharp pain in his thigh. The little girl had attached herself to his leg, gnawing through the denim of his jeans, seeking out the life-giving flesh beneath. He knocked her away and started to run again, but had gone no more than two paces when bony hands exploded from the mud and gripped his ankles.

Around him the marsh bubbled and heaved as figures emerged from its depths. Pale, skeletal figures, their parchment skin streaked with earth and weed. Ten, twenty of them, rising from the mud pools to stand, surrounding him.

He looked back at Louise imploringly, but she hadn't moved and her face was impassive. Next to her stood the boy he'd discovered in the shed, flour white and spindle thin. His impossibly thin body draped incongruously in Louise's waxed jacket. He was smiling, his white skin almost glinting in the late afternoon sun, as Louise draped a maternal arm across his shoulders.

Dusk was drawing in over the verdant expanse of Flatland Marsh, coating the swaying figures with a deathly paleness that began to mask them from view. In the barely visible distance Tom could just about make out more thin figures, bleached of colour as if washed up on a shore, swaying like reeds over the flat land.

Louise was all but invisible now, and as Tom looked down at his own body he realised that he too was losing all his natural colour; becoming as one with the children of the marsh.

First published in the collection *Falling Into Heaven*. Sarob Press 2004.

Cash Cow

Hroubadour Tusk

Jack's success with the beanstalk triggered a gold rush in the magic bean industry. Most farmers had at least one low-performing cow they were willing to trade. They just hadn't ever considered bringing back gold from a kingdom in the sky to be a realistic option.

Horace was shrewd enough to know that conquering giants, winning riches, tales of glory were never going to be his destiny. His name was Horace. It just wasn't what heroes were called. Stories like that were reserved for your Jacks, your Cinderellas, your Charmings.

Horace thought it was cheating to name your son "Charming."

Instead Horace became one of the first traders to cater to this new bean-buying market. Magic beans were the perfect product: beans so light and easy to come by and magic being such a usefully vague term. It was the stroke of fortune Horace felt he deserved. Jack's giant had fallen on his house. Horace felt justified in raising funds for the repairs however he could.

He knew nothing about magic beans, but knew everything there was to know about telling customers why the shortcomings of their recent purchase were their fault and not his. Once the beans ran out, it didn't take much to persuade desperate buyers to accept a magic carrot, a magic pebble, a magic button. It was an excellent way to get rid of clutter around the house.

With all the items being sold as magical, one or two genuine articles were bound to slip through the cracks.

Gunk had been leaking from the walls of Horace's house ever since the giant fell, yet once more Horace had weaved success from personal misfortune. Shaping it to look like more magic beans, he had sold it on to Muriel Happenhard. He disliked Muriel. Not for anything she had done personally, but because of a talking cow she owned. Horace felt the animal looked down its nose at him, refusing to ever say a word in his presence. This wasn't great for Horace's self-esteem.

* * *

Muriel had no intention of climbing up into the clouds herself. There was enough to be getting on with down here. The beans were for her fiancé.

She was running out of ideas to delay the wedding. She'd tried feigning madness. It had been fun for a while, but she'd had to drop it when it became clear he planned to marry her anyway and abandon her to an asylum. She'd staked a lifetime of service aboard a pirate ship on a dice game but ended up accidentally winning the pot.

If a beanstalk grew in her back garden, her fiancé would have to climb. If he refused, he would be branded a coward and her father would cancel the engagement. If he climbed, maybe he would like it up there and want to stay.

If not, she had her axe.

But now there was another problem. She rapped on Horace's door, ignoring the "Do Not Disturb" sign. She assumed an "except for Muriel" was implied, as she did with most instructions she disliked.

"It's the magic beans you sold me," she blurted out as he opened the door. "They're broken."

She was ready to pay him to identify the problem but hadn't expected him to ask for Fowler in exchange. She loved her talking cow. They had grown up together. It was Muriel who had taught Fowler to speak.

Though perhaps she was being selfish. Fowler rarely spoke these days and Muriel blamed herself. She knew she wasn't exactly stimulating conversation. Maybe Fowler needed a new owner, someone with whom she could really debate. Horace was an intelligent man, a worldly man. Selling Fowler to him could solve a problem for them both. Muriel agreed to Horace's terms and showed him to where the beans were planted. She clutched her one remaining bean – her last hope – tightly in her fist.

"It didn't look right to me." She watched his face closely as he gazed into the gaping hole that had appeared in the night, exactly where she had planted the bean.

She grew uncomfortable with the silence as Horace examined the hole. A terrible thought urged her to jump in and see where it ended. She was brought back to reality by Fowler, who had come to see what was going on, licking her hand. Muriel patted her friend affectionately and felt the warmth of Fowler's tongue cover her palm.

After what seemed like forever, Horace straightened up and looked her in the eye.

"You've planted it upside down."

A "moo" came from above, shaking the earth. Muriel turned to see Fowler rising into the sky, 10 feet tall and still growing.

* * *

Though she could talk, Fowler couldn't hear. After all the time Muriel had spent teaching her the language, Fowler had been embarrassed to find herself going deaf just as she approached fluency. In darker moments she believed she was being punished for her hubris.

She had decided to avoid conversation altogether. It saved her the humiliation of saying the wrong thing because she hadn't heard what had come before. Cows can't lip read.

Fowler did not like the look of that hole. Not at all. She ambled over to Muriel and licked her hand to reassure her that everything would be okay as long as neither of them went near that hole. There was something small and squishy in Muriel's palm. Fowler ate it, assuming that was what it was for. Now she looked down at her legs and saw them expanding rapidly.

Alas, thought Fowler, *what cruel misfortune hath befallen me this time.* Her head passed through a cloud. As the chill moved through her ear, Fowler suddenly realised she could hear birdsong with perfect clarity. Maybe she could enjoy this.

Just as she started to worry about getting too high, she stopped growing. She shuffled her hooves outwards to stop herself toppling. She was eye-level with the moon. Fowler had never seen the moon before. She thought she could reach it, maybe even exceed it.

She took a few steps back, preparing to jump.

Her weight left the ground and she started to soar. She stretched to touch the moon as it passed her by below. She somersaulted her way past an astonished spaceship manned by a species yet to encounter either humans or cows. *I'll worry about landing*, she thought, *when I'm on my way down*.

Frank

Paul Walker

Frank is a homeless person. He is at least 60 years old and has survived on the streets of West London for over 20 years. His domain is restricted to an area within a boundary formed by imaginary lines running from Marble Arch to Marylebone Station, Tavistock Square and the Aldwych. He regards himself as a cut above those that hang out around Mile End and New Cross. He's an educated man, or claims to be, and one of his pleasures in life is using complicated words in conversation or shouting them randomly at the drivers of cars which park inconsiderately or untidily in 'his' streets. Many of his favourite words come from three books which were acquired as park bench discards and he now keeps securely packed away in a favourite rucksack which he calls Jessica. The books are *Carry On, Jeeves, A Short History of Gyrocopters* and *Formica: A Technical Appreciation.* He has assimilated all the impressive words in these books without necessarily understanding them.

Frank's constant companion is Truncheon, an eight-year-old, toffee-coloured mongrel of melancholy disposition. His previous dog was also named Truncheon and possibly the one before that, although he can't be certain. Recently, Frank has noticed that the winter nights are getting colder and darker. His dreams are filled with images of log fires, the soft touch of eiderdowns and the smell of marmite, thickly spread on hot, buttered toast. He is also troubled at the realisation that his beard is getting longer, his field of vision shorter and visits to a toilet (or similar) more frequent. In summary, Frank is unsettled.

One early morning in January as he is folding away his bedding, he notices an advertisement in *The Lady* magazine. Frank swears there is extra cushion and comfort in the pages of the better class of women's magazines and often selects *The Lady* or *Vogue* for pillow duty. The advertisement calls for a Warden/Housekeeper at Kiplin Hall, a popular tourist attraction in North Yorkshire. Duties listed appear light and include security, safety, cleaning and assisting in the tea rooms. Best of all, the job comes with a live-in cottage. He reads the advert several times and feels a warm cosiness spreading through his body as an idea takes hold. He will apply for the position. After all, he reasons, he's from London and he's likely to be the only applicant willing to move from the bright lights and sophistication of the capital to a North Yorkshire backwater.

Frank goes to a café on Goodge Street to seek the help of his friend, Lionel, who has a job in the kitchen. Lionel agrees that a 'live-in' cottage is likely to have a log fire and at least one eiderdown. A 'live-out' cottage, on the other hand, may be less welcoming. He encourages Frank to apply, finds him paper, an envelope and seats him at a table. Progress is slow as Frank chooses his words carefully, often seeking confirmation of a well-turned phrase from Lionel, customers and Truncheon. Finally, late in the afternoon, the letter of application is completed.

THE LETTER

Dear Lord and Lady Kiplin

I want to be your warden and housekeeper at Kiplin Hall.

I am an urbane man based in the classiest part of London, but I have a fondness for the countryside up north and used to own a pair of green wellington boots. I speak BBC English and am willing to learn a second language quickly until I am perfectly affluent.

I have worked in several jobs including insurance, lumberjacking and Club18-30 Rep. I have had many duties including writing, algebra, chopping wood, drinking and cleaning toilets. All these were performed economically and with due perfection.

First, to the warden bit. I realise that to be a true warden I will need a tin helmet and whistle. I promise to obtain same before travelling up north. And finally, security, which I am good at, through being strong, having a loud voice and forbidding appearance.

In your tea room I can honestly claim to be an expert in the provision of combustibles and associated snacks. I strongly urge you to replace old wooden tables and chairs with a new material that has great flexural strength and eminent cleanability. Of course, I mention Formica, which will not trap germs and spread terrible diseases among your customers. Please take this advice as a free opening gamble.

But pardon me, I digest. On to the main topic of cleaning and housekeeping - I will be superb and am the proud owner of an apron with the interesting incorporation of fake female breasts. (This is strictly non-offensive to the paying public.) I handle brushes with both my right and left hands with ample dexterity.

To end this compendium, I must add that I already feel a strong intimacy with you having eaten many thousands of your fine cakes. Even the out of date ones taste finger-licking good. My favourite is Bakewell tart and bottom of my list (but still very good) is Victoria sponge. You can probably tell that I'm an entrepreneur of cakes with my fabled sweet tooth.

My last requirement is an easy one. I need an eiderdown, log fire and easy access to a flushing toilet.

Your humble servant
Frank Beaurepair (of that ilk)

P.S. I will be clean, presentable and honest in due course. I only ever consider non-smoking doorways and underpasses.

Lights

Chris Rawlins

It was quite a typical autumn day in Surrey – cool and sunny with the prospect of sundown a bit earlier than we were used to during most of our season. As village cricketers in the southern part of Surrey, we played local villages in northern Hampshire for an annual league trophy. Plus the runners-up had to provide a night-out for the winners in late October.

This year our village team from Downside was playing a team from Headley in Hampshire in the final game of the year to decide the champions and runners-up. Headley batted first and made an impressive 169 for 8 from their allocated forty overs. As we started our innings, I had a premonition that something strange might happen. It was clouding over with some grey clouds making the pitch look darker than earlier in the afternoon. With this extra handicap, our openers got off to a terrific start teaching 103 before we lost our first wicket. From then on, we were definitely a "downside". We lost so many wickets that we crashed down to 166 for 7 in the space of only an hour since losing our first batsman.

By this time, the light had become so poor that the umpires determined that it was "not cricket" to continue and they suspended play. The bowlers could hardly see anything and our batsmen certainly couldn't see the Headley fast bowlers starting their run-up. So that was it for the day, and the season. As the umpires walked off, the Headley fielding team ran towards the pavilion, and there they were – lights! All this active running had triggered a collection of motion light sensors scattered around the field, located in the grounds of Farnham Castle. The effect was dramatic. At first, nobody could believe it but then our tail-enders hurried back to their creases. The fielders and bowler had no option but to take their positions. The umpires soon realised that there was a necessity for them to rejoin them and let play resume.

But this was only possible if enough players were actually moving. The first ball bowled under these floodlights went so fast and wide that it missed our batsman, the wicket, and the wicketkeeper on the leg side by yards. As it crossed the boundary for 4 byes, we had won!

Acknowledging our victory, the Downside captain raced on to the field, shouting:

"Lights – thank you, we've won".

A voice from the crowd yelled, "But No Camera!"

At that point, the entire Downside team screamed, "But plenty of Action!"

Lord and Lady Moneytree

Charlotte McDermott

L ord and Lady Moneytree were sitting in the rose garden drinking tea. It was quite a cold day but the sky was blue and the roses were so beautiful at this time of year, it seemed an awful shame to sit indoors. Lady Moneytree carefully placed the blanket around her husband legs, she should hate for him to get a chill. He stared ahead of him as if engrossed in what he was reading. His one-armed spectacles rested on his nose at a jaunty angle, this morning's breakfast still lingering on his beard. She kissed his forehead.

Lady Moneytree carefully picked up her cup, it didn't have a handle and so she had to wait until it was cool enough to touch. Lord Moneytree shook out his Financial Times importantly. It was upside down and two months old but Lady Moneytree did not mention that.

'Is there any cake Fluffy? I am rather peckish.'

Lady Moneytree suspected there wasn't any cake but she picked up the bell and jangled it anyway.

It was some time before she saw Edna come trudging across the garden. Edna's apron was covered in brown marks and she had clearly rubbed her face with whatever it was and was looking somewhat dishevelled.

'Is there any cake Edna?'

'What kind of cake Ma'am?'

'Any kind will do.'

'I don't think there is but I am sure I could find some biscuits.'

'That would be lovely Edna, thank you.'

Edna trundled back over the grass, chuntering to herself on the way as she so often did.

'I say Fluffy, it's a shame about the roses.'

'What do you mean? They're lovely.'

'Well yes, apart from the ones that Eddie has been at... running around with his stick again I shouldn't wonder....that boy!'

Lady Moneytree smiled weakly and looked down at her saucer. She squeezed her eyes tightly but still one tear managed to bravely escape and plop delicately into her saucer.

* * *

'You look so smart Eddie and terribly handsome.'

'Now Mother, you're not going to get all teary on me.'

'Of course not, as if I would!'

'My train leaves at quarter past, so I really should be making a move.'

'Oh but I asked Edna to make you some supper and your Father will want to see you.'

'I really want to make this train Ma, otherwise I shan't be travelling with the other boys.'

'I thought he would be back by now, he'll be so disappointed not to see you off.'

'We said our goodbyes this morning, I'll be back in no time...you'll see.'

* * *

'I think we should be going inside now Darling, it's getting a bit nippy and I felt rain.'

'Oh but I thought we were having cake.'

'We had biscuits... don't you remember? Come along now let's get you inside.'

Lady Moneytree held out her hand to her husband who held her hand obediently; ready to be lead inside.

'Do you know Fluffy, I really am looking forward to the holidays.'

'Holidays?'

'School holidays.'

'Oh?'

'Get Eddie back, sort out his fast bowl.'

'Yes Darling.'

Lady Moneytree settled her husband into his favourite armchair. He closed his eyes and sighed a long deep sigh.

Without opening his eyes he reached for her and held her arm for a moment.

'I didn't get to say goodbye.'

'I know Darling...I know.'

Edna was in the drawing room, placing a bucket under a leak, muttering to herself. Lady Moneytree glanced around at the faded carpet and the sad peeling walls. The sunflowers were a pale sickly yellow; they seemed tired and helpless.

'It's getting worse Ma'am I've already filled one bucket.'

'I am sorry Edna, it's all rather a mess isn't it?'

'I am not sure how much longer this can go on Ma'am.'

'No Edna, neither am I.'

Summer

David Strong

I was chosen because I have a gift with arithmetic. I am good at logic problems and have a methodical, tangential attitude to solving mathematical formula and equations. I have an empathy and a propensity with numbers and sums. Add to that the ability to speak three foreign languages... yeah... so what? But generally I am useless. People irritate and bore me. I have never had a regular job, have always struggled to pay my way. I have no inclination to teach and even research has become tedious. My name is Luke. Nobody likes me. I'm too intense, too stuck up, too introspective.

I know and I really do not care. I don't care how I dress, about personal hygiene, my hair, my filthy nails. The superficiality of it all bores me. I have never had a regular job, I have struggled to pay my way, I have no inclination to teach and even research has become tedious.

Yet here I am.

I have left my little one-bedroomed apartment on West-side, I no longer have to worry about the domestic chores of everyday life and I am looked after. Among friends, well, I am part of a team; that in itself is interesting... not that I have a choice...

The world is building up to some sort of biblical kind of Armageddon. War, earthquake, famine, disease. I am almost relieved to be able to concentrate on something complicated enough to take my mind and my thoughts away.

* * *

There was a knock on the door and a man in uniform telling me what to do. Within days I was whisked away to this simple office, this chalet within a compound. Hidden away secretly. I am no longer allowed spontaneous communication, all of my mails are censored, not that I get a lot... I am forbidden to tell anybody about the job we are doing... hey!... that we have been kidnapped here to do. But what do I care? Nobody really worries about me; father gave up on me ages ago. He said that I had wasted my talents. And he is right. Do I see this as an opportunity to prove myself? No. This is just another dead end. But at least it is a worthy challenge.

* * *

The task is complicated and we are not getting any nearer a resolution. But there is an occasional probably misplaced enthusiasm and energy amongst us that, occasionally gives us hope. We just need a breakthrough. A moment of inspiration.

Let's face it, the world outside the confines of this place is getting crazier, we often talk about the politics of it all and where we are going with this project. We have no doubt in it is probably vital to the future of mankind, that might sound sensational but it is a reasonable statement. Hey. No pressure then...

* * *

Whilst part of the world sinks beneath the melting ice caps, whilst humanity struggles violently against itself and greed and selfishness rules, whilst society stands of the precipice of collapse, whilst we spend more money on creating weapons than clearing up the mess than using weapons create, whilst we spend more energy on personal entertainment than work and whilst we leave half of the world struggling to eat and to survive. We will slip back into neolithism. It makes me sick and bereft.

* * *

There are a team of us working on the project. We are all similar misfits, similar supposed geniuses or gifted analysts. We are referred to as the summers, but we are past caring what they call us. Two months in and we are not the slightest bit nearer to the interpretation, translation, understanding and decoding of a series of messages. I know what they expect of us. But the task is impossible, ridiculous and hopeless. There is no such thing as a universal translator. The whole concept of any alien life being similar to us is ludicrous. They used to say life depends on three basics: oxygen, light and water... baloney! We are completely blinkered because we only see our insular Earth set up. The whole concept has been blown apart. What we accept as intelligence is negotiable. We have a multitude of intelligent animals, fish and birds here on Earth – we have now found similar even in our solar system: basic forms of life... and suspect other systems have intelligence but there is such a difference. We cannot talk to dolphins – how are we supposed to talk to sentient beings from Rigel4?

* * *

The Hildebrand legacy pays us. But the payment we are forced to pay in is secrecy... whose wealth was amassed in the creation of fusion energy that revolutionised the post caliphate wars...

They have turned to us, our group of misfits simply because the computer programmers have thrown their arms up and admitted defeat. Quantum mechanics: no problem, molecule modelling: easy, space travel: pah!! Computers with megaPFLOPS based in Tokyo... they used time on even the IBM super computer, secretly of course, but it could not come up with a solution. Of course, we are not surprised. Since the worldwide crash in the early 22nd Century that caused global panic and destabilisation and power blackouts that lasted long enough to kill nearly 2 million, the world has ceased to believe that advanced computers and robots will solve and eradicate every problem from poverty to global warming, from disease to natural disasters.

* * *

This is the most pressing, most important of problems. A series of numbers that need deciphering, but it is more than that. It is much more. You wouldn't understand. Try and imagine an octillion pulses of light in wave spectral oscillations, a stream of coloured signal bursts in different forms and intensity. It is more a jigsaw that needs making than a code that needs breaking. Why important? It is secret and cannot remain secret. Nothing this big remains a real secret. There have been media whispers about if for decades; but it is an enigma and until we know what it means, if it means anything, what it says, if it says anything; hell, it might just be a random beacon set up by a star-travelling alien race, it might possibly be a natural black hole phenomena. But.

It might also be a hello. An introduction to a civilised species that could befriend us, offer us technology and give us, the human race a new perspective.

* * *

But we cannot read it. We have no idea. Perhaps we are not ready. Perhaps we are not deserving. Perhaps we will never know. Who knows?

Life Lines

Caroline Markovitch

"**M**rs Davidson, Welcome to Bellevue Spa. My name's Shannon and I'll be your therapist today. It's a pleasure to have you with us." The orange tinted woman, her hair scraped into a high, shiny bun spoke in a sing-song voice that was both patronising and insincere in equal measure.

"Thank you, it's nice to be here. I'm so excited, I've never been to a spa before."

"Ah, yes," oozed Shannon, looking her up and down, "You're one of our competition winners – Glamorous Grandmother isn't it?"

"Er, no..." Beth blushed, unsure why she was the one feeling embarrassed. "Actually it was a gift from my sister. I've been having a bit of a tough time recently."

"Oh goodness, yes of course... Please forgive me. We get so many people and I didn't mean to imply..." She seemed to run out of steam, as if the effort of apologising was just too much. Then, fixing her whitened smile on her over-tightened face she continued brightly. "Well...yes, anyway, please come through to the Zen Lounge and make yourself at home. Have a little browse through our treatment list and I'll be back in a few minutes to talk through what you'd like."

Shannon and her rather oppressive perfume swept out of the room, leaving Beth to enjoy the tinkling spa music and mood lighting. The walls were painted in muted, natural tones and the air was delicately scented with something exotic and calming. She sank into the soft white sofa feeling that this was about as far from her normal life as it was possible to be.

Beth reflected that perhaps her sister had been right, things had been tough recently and she did need a break. With redundancy from the job she had worked hard at for 20 years, more time spent looking after her increasingly frail mum, and her two boisterous teenage boys, always asking her to drive them somewhere or cook them something; there was no doubt that she could do with a bit of pampering.

As she flicked through the treatment menu Beth was baffled by the variety of ways available to be preened, plumped (and presumably pruned) all for a hefty price. It looked rather intimidating, and if she was honest most of it made no sense at all. She didn't fancy an 'Organic Mud and Banana Facial', whatever that was, and she couldn't imagine any possible scenario where a 'Warm Cucumber Colonic Irrigation' would seem like a relaxing idea.

An older couple sauntered through the lounge, enveloped in matching fluffy white robes and little slippers, while a group of younger women sat sipping fruit teas and chatting in the corner.

Why did they all look so relaxed and calm? More to the point, why did she feel so stressed and tense? It was just a new experience, she told herself. She wasn't used to being pampered and treated.

She picked up another leaflet, one with a picture of a serene beauty on the front, just as Shannon appeared at her shoulder.

"Ooh, Botox – an excellent choice, it will give you just the lift you need."

"Oh, I wasn't looking at that..." Beth protested, wondering how this awful woman was able to keep insulting her without appearing to care. "It was just...."

"No need to be embarrassed," Shannon interrupted briskly, "We all need a little bit of help now and then and we could sort those lines and wrinkles out in no time. Not to mention the crow's feet and those little creases around your mouth," she added, clearly warming to her theme.

"I think I'd just like a shoulder massage or maybe a facial," Beth suggested tentatively.

"Oh yes, we have a lovely facial designed just for the older woman – perfect for smoothing ageing skin and brightening a dull complexion. Shall we get started?"

Beth gathered her things and prepared to follow but suddenly stopped. "Could you point me in the direction of the loos?"

"Certainly, the restroom is first on the left. Just come to Treatment Room 3 when you're done."

A few minutes later Beth stood under the harsh fluorescent lights of the ladies toilets, resting her forehead against the cool glass mirror. Then, drawing herself upright she raked her hair back from her face with her fingers.

She stared at her reflection, taking in every crease and crinkle that had appeared without her really noticing.

Perhaps she did need a bit of help. Maybe she should hand herself over to professionals so her face could be scrubbed clean of all those imperfections.

Then she stopped.

She looked closer.

Those lines and wrinkles were part of her. They represented each worry, trauma, care and trouble that had crossed her life. But they were also from the laughter that crinkled the corners of her eyes, the smiles she shared with her children, the kisses, the tears and the joy that had filled her 47 years on Earth.

She realised her face had grown with her and told the story of her life so far. Why would she want that erased? Why would she want Shannon and her needle wielding posse to freeze her expression or plump her lips, scouring her skin clean of the experiences, both good and bad, that had combined to make her everything she was today?

She left the Ladies and marched over to Treatment Room 3.

"Ah, Mrs Davidson, come in and let's see what we can do with that face"

"Actually, Shannon, I won't be needing your 'help', today or ever. I love my face - wrinkles and all. I don't care if people see that I'm getting older and just because my face isn't full of chemicals doesn't mean I'm less of a woman. I'm sure you'll find plenty of ladies who want to rub away the years, but not me. I'm happy just the way I am."

With that, she swept from the room feeling lighter and taller than she had in months.

Maybe there was something in this spa experience after all.

Kismet

Emma Branch

How did I meet my second husband? Well there's a story and a half there. As you know, Ted and I spilt up what, 10-15 years ago, around the time Simon left home for Uni. It wasn't really anybody's fault, we just grew up and grew apart. We were both so focused on work and our own interests that without Simon we found we had nothing to hold us together anymore. For a long time I really was OK on my own. Simon was always popping home to fill the freezer and get his washing done and my Mum was quite unwell for the last few years, so I suppose I was busy and my life was full. The change from being alone to being lonely didn't really hit me until I turned 50. Mum passed away and Simon emigrated to Australia. With time on my hands it finally hit me like a slap in the face. A voice in my head started shouting "wake up, is this what you want? Do you plan to be alone for the next 40 years of your life?"

I decided to be brave and dropped into conversation at work that I might like to meet someone but didn't know how. The youngsters thought it was a hoot. Well they actually said it was "sick" which at first I took to mean they were revolted, but apparently it means it's cool, especially considering my great age and obvious impending death. They fell about laughing at the thought of me on Tinder, no not Grinder, apparently that's something quite different. But then they suggested I register with dating sites called Plenty of Fish, My Best Friend and Find a Sugar Daddy. How old a sugar daddy would have to be for a crone like me, was discussed in hushed tones!

During a lunch break they set me up on a reputable site, rewrote my profile, skimmed 10 years off my age, 10 lbs off my weight and rejected the nice photo of me with Simon at Mum's funeral for a photoshopped selfie. When I saw my bio I didn't recognise myself. I was quite fanciable! I didn't know that I ran marathons and regularly worked out at the gym. Volunteering at the charity shop was replaced with a fundraising walk along the Great Wall of China with accompanying photos. It was so convincing I began to believe it despite the fact the closest I'd been to China was the local take away. I swear to God, their talents were wasted in that call centre.

I was warned off using my real name, so I assumed what they described as my Porn Star name. That's the name of my pet and the first word in my street. Pixie Willow went live on the site that weekend, not resembling me at all. She was obviously quite a catch and soon attracted a lot of attention.

The kids at work whittled out the timewasters and weirdos and left me with a chap who called himself ETB123. His profile picture was of a boarder terrier, his profile said he had returned to the UK after working abroad a year ago, he had 2 children, a dog and was recently divorced.

We emailed a couple of times, he seemed nice, but reserved. The kids at work told me to skip to the meet up quickly, don't let him string out the messaging and certainly don't meet anyone who sends a picture of their... I took their advice and bit the bullet. In the third message I asked if he wanted to meet up. He did! He lived fairly close so we arranged that I'd book a table at my favourite restaurant, Kismet, which thankfully he was familiar with.

I walked into the bar feeling like a cross between a right twit and a right tart. A couple of the girls in the office had taken me clothes shopping and had dumped me in the beauty salon. I felt a little bit more like Pixie Willow, but the gaps in the story still worried me. They said don't worry, everyone tells a few porkies on their profile. I felt we were pushing the boundaries of what a few porkies were to the pig farm and back again.

I gave my real name to the barman for the table booking. A chap standing at the bar with his back towards me turned around and blow me down, I couldn't believe it; there stood my ex-husband, Ted. I prayed that the ground would open and swallow me up. After an initial awkward greeting I explained I was on a date and he told me he was waiting for a friend. I felt like a complete idiot, embarrassed, as if I had been caught cheating, even though we'd split up a lifetime ago. There was nothing else to do but chat whilst we waited for our respective companions. Simon had kept our lives with him very separate, I hadn't realised how much so, and we soon talked easily about him, his new life in Melbourne and what had happened to each of us over the years. It was only when I finished my glass of wine that I realised my date hadn't turned up. I excused myself to powder my nose and check my phone. The last message from ETB123 said he was looking forward to seeing me at 7:30. Bastard! He'd probably got a better offer from a real 41 year old with a real 28 inch waist.

I went back out, Ted was standing by the bar looking at his phone. "It looks like my date's not coming," I announced picking up my new coat. "It was lovely seeing you again."

"Hang on," he interrupted, "My friend's running late or got caught up or something, did you say you had a table booked? I don't know about you but I'm starving, it would be a shame to waste it... if you want?"

"Yes, yes it's been great catching up and I would love to have dinner, if you want to, if you are sure your friend isn't coming." It was true, I was having fun. It was just like the best of old times. I'd forgotten how much I liked him.

His hand felt familiar in the small of my back as he guided me towards the table. "I won't be a minute," he smiled. "I'd better let my friend know I got a better offer." He winked at me in the way that always made me smile and walked back towards the bar. As the waiter brought the menus over my phone pinged. The message read, "Hi Pixie, sorry to let you down but I just re-met the girl of my dreams."

Ding Dong on High

Chris Rawlins

My name is Ben. No, not Big Ben in London; he just sits around a load of useless politicians who only work for about twenty weeks in the year. I am actually a large Ben who has resided in the tower of St Michaels's Church in Melbourne (Derbyshire, not Australia) for over two centuries. I am the biggest bell and am surrounded by eight smaller and younger bells. We get along very well together and don't fall out or make a lot of noise – most of the time. However, every Sunday some humans come along and pull our ropes. We make a lot of noise then until plenty of other humans join them. They then leave us alone and start singing or talking. They also make some other signs until at some point, having sipped a silver cup of red wine, they then stagger off and leave us alone. Perhaps later on the same day they may come back and the whole process is repeated.

Being the biggest and oldest, I always have the last laugh. My younger siblings usually start jingling in a tuneful manner until I join in to add some base tone. Then they all stop until somebody looks up at me and sings:

"Do be quiet, Ben, we're ready to start the service."

I reply with a number of clangs until the lead ringer, Rodney, ties his rope to one of the church pillars.

But Sunday is not the only day we get excited and send out a happy tune. On some other days of the week we are called into action at various times for different reasons. One regular event happens on a Wednesday evening, except during the summer holidays in August. It's rather boring actually because our individual bell ringers just pull on our ropes. There is nobody else in the church – not even the vicar. They do this for about two hours although I am puzzled as to why. Unless, of course, they wish us to simply annoy the local residents who are enjoying an evening drink in their gardens during the summer, or watching television at other times of the year. We can certainly make a lot of noise when we get going with our ropes being pulled hard and fast.

On some other days during the week, we may get called into action at various times. Usually once a week, the church fills with people before a large wooden box is brought into the nave. I am often the only bell that is asked to dong while the vicar blesses the life of a fallen man or woman with these final words:

"May she (or he) rest in peace."

It seems so sad that I am the only bell who is asked to make a dong. These people have done wonderful deeds during their life and we should all be allowed to thank them in our own way. Over the years, I have heard of people who have been shot in overseas battles, been killed in a car accident, died from a dreadful illness, old age, or simply fallen into the sea, fallen out of a plane, fallen out of a skyscraper, or fallen off a ladder. These are all such sad occasions but I seem to have outlived them all.

Perhaps our happiest and most glorious event only takes place on a few Saturdays each year. The church is packed with people from all age groups, and with flowers and decorations everywhere. All the women and girls are dressed up in bright-coloured gowns and wearing enormous hats and glamorous jewelry. On the contrary, all the boys and men are dressed up in boring white shirts and black suits, most of which look as if they have been cut to avoid the front getting messed up. Then one old man enters the church with a young woman on his arm after we are all exhausted from a very hectic, lengthy and loud period of jingling. Afterwards, a younger man joins the young woman in front of the vicar; they all exchange some words before the vicar proclaims:

"I pronounce you as husband and wife. Those whom God has joined together in holy matrimony, let no man put asunder."

Then this happy couple walk the whole length of the church's aisle with hand in hand. The organ continues to play while my friends and I make the loudest dingles of our lives. It is a truly remarkable occasion, not only for us, but also every single person in the church, especially those leading the procession. I hope it really is the happiest day of their lives. It certainly is for me – and I have seen almost 75,000 of them. But I am only a bell – and a big one at that, dinging up on high.

Auxilium Sui

Alan Davie

Martin loved books. The content was unimportant; he loved the look, the feel, even the smell of a book, especially if it was old. He had a small collection and was always on the look-out for more. This was why he was in a gloomy, small second-hand bookshop on a sunny day in a sea-side town.

The shopkeeper was keeping a close eye on the small boy browsing through his stock and became more vigilant as the boy stood on tip-toes and removed a small volume from a shelf.

"Can I help you," he asked.

The boy seemed to be caressing the book but had not opened it.

"It's beautiful," the boy replied.

The shopkeeper admired the boy's taste; he knew that book well and agreed that the leather binding with an inlayed art-deco design was indeed beautiful.

"It was written by a retired Oxford Don who lived locally, it was published in 1922. It was intended as a self-help guide, for soldiers returning from the Great War."

Realising that one so young might not understand he continued, "That is the First World War, 1914-1918. Thousands of soldiers were slaughtered, and the few who survived were disturbed by what had happened to them; they found it hard to adjust to civilian life."

Martin listened intently, eager for more, the book still cradled in his hands.

The shopkeeper, pleased to have an attentive audience, continued.

"The book was written in simple language and contained some sensible, if somewhat patronising, advice. If it had been sold in a cheap paperback form, it would have been a great success, but for some reason, it was published as the book you hold in your hand. The price put it out of the reach of most people and it was a complete failure."

Martin thanked the shopkeeper for telling him so much, looked lovingly at the book, ran his hand over it, raised it to his nose and then stood on his tip-toes to return it to the shelf.

"I thought you wanted that book," said the shopkeeper

"I do, but I can't afford it. The sign says 'all books on this shelf £1'. I only have 67p."

The shopkeeper, recognising a fellow bibliophile, said, "We might be able to negotiate, but first you must tell me about yourself."

"My name is Martin Daniels; I am 9years and 10months old. We, that's, me, my Dad and my sister are here on holiday.

We are staying at Aunty Jane's house, it's a really big house, she is married to Uncle Bill, he is a bookmaker, but I don't think he could make a book as beautiful as this."

The shopkeeper smiled at this, but said, "What about your mother?" and immediately regretted it, for the boy's eyes filled with tears.

"My Mum was very ill. She went to hospital. I never saw her again. She died."

The shopkeeper was devastated at causing the boy so much grief, he wanted to give him a hug but realised it would be inappropriate. "I am so sorry," he said. "What about your sister?" To his surprise this meek little boy with tears still running down his cheeks turned into an angry, yapping, terrier.

"Mandy? I hate her. She's fourteen. She thinks she's a princess. She made me give her my pocket money, so I can't buy that book. She calls me 'Worm'. I hate her."

"Hey! OK! She doesn't sound very nice, but I'm sure she isn't too bad and remember she is family. That book in your hand stresses that family is very important. Why does she call you 'Worm'?"

"Oh! I don't know, I think it's because Dad called me a bookworm, once."

"On thinking about it, that book might have a lot of good advice for you. In a way, you are like those poor soldiers. You have been through a traumatic experience and have lost a friend, your Mum. You no longer have to mindlessly obey your sister. You have to build a new life in which you are in charge."

The shopkeeper settled down to skim through the book, and point out advice that could be relevant to Martin. After half an hour, Martin was feeling much happier and more confident. He thanked the shopkeeper and made to return the book to its place on the shelf.

"I have just remembered, we have a sale on today, everything is half price." The shopkeeper lied. "You can have that book for 50p."

"Really! Oh, thank you, it is so lovely, are you sure?"

"Of course I'm sure," said the shopkeeper, thinking he would be happy to sell all the remaining copies of that book at that price. He had at least ten in his store room, left over from the Author's house clearance.

"Thank you again, and thank you for the advice. It's getting late. We are going home and I must meet Dad in the car-park." Looking lovingly at his new possession, he reached the door, turned and asked "What does this mean on the spine 'AUXILIUM SUI'?"

"It's Latin and translates as Self-help, most inappropriate for a book like that."

Martin made his way down the alley that leads to the sea-front repeating to himself 'Auxilium Sui', 'Auxilium Sui'. At the junction with another alley Martin looked to the right and saw his sister with a local boy, he was pushing Mandy against the wall and was trying to pour beer from a can down her throat.

"Get that inside you, Posh, then we'll see what you're really like."

Martin could see that she was not happy, no longer the confident princess, despite the fact that she had a cigarette in her fingers. He raised the book in the air and shouted "AUXILIUM SUI."

The words bounced off the alley walls giving a weird echo affect. The boy was temporarily stunned to see a small being casting a spell on him. Mandy wriggled free and ran towards her brother.

"Car–park!" he told her.

He repeated the Latin phrase as loudly as possible, but the boy was beginning to realise what was happening and started menacingly towards Martin. Martin turned and ran after his sister. Luckily the car-park was fairly close and their father was there waiting for them.

"There's no need to rush, you are only five minutes late."

"Sorry," said Mandy, panting, "We didn't know what the time was"

"Where have you been? What is that smell?"

"A boy squirted a can of beer at Mandy," Martin replied

"And Martin saved me."

They had both spotted the boy lumbering after them, and had also seen him slink away when he saw their Dad, who was tall and broad.

"It all sounds a bit strange. Mandy, you will have to change, but not here. We will stop at the Service Station on the Motorway, you can change there. We really must get going and get out of town before the rush hour."

Brother and sister slipped into the back seat of the car and fastened their seat belts. Mandy whispered, "Thank you, bookworm," and smiled as she returned his two pound pocket money. "What's the book?"

"It is a Self-help book and it really works."

Disappear

Charlotte McDermott

'Ladies and Gentlemen, please put your hands together for the amazing Jason O'Donnelly and his gorgeous assistant Janette.'

The audience clapped their hands and whistled through their rough lips. Fat bums shuffled their way down aisles avoiding the sticky soup that lay there. It had been a good night at Croydon Working Men's Club. The beer was flat but cheap and there was no shortage of KP peanuts.

'I have no idea how she came out in one piece,' said the barmaid June artfully balancing her fag on one lip as she dried up a pint glass.

'They was real swords and swords are dead sharp,' said Billy her son with great authority.

'Bloody good turn tonight June, I thought we'd never see that Jack of 'arts again, and then it turns up inside a lemon,' chimed Stan slurping the dregs of his pint and lapping back the milky foam that now adorned his moustache.

'Yeah, but when he opened the box, she weren't there,' said Billy proud once again of his powers of observation.

'Bloody brilliant!' declared Stan as he struggled to keep both bottom cheeks on the stool at the same time.

'Glad you enjoyed it!' Jason O'Donnelly stepped into the adoring crowd and grinned playfully at the barmaid.

'Quick one for the road?'

'You bet and then I'll see if I can squeeze in a pint.'

Stan and Billy tittered 'Ooh you cheeky thing,' said June as her ash slipped into his pint.

Janette was folding away the costumes into the trunk. She had a system for all their gadgets and contraptions, which required careful folding and taking apart and fitting into the trunk. Jason never helped put anything away; he claimed he didn't know where it went. She would have to drag him away from the bar she thought as she dragged the trunk outside and through the slimy car park. It was tipping it down, the rain slapped her in the face and she felt the sting.

He had scratched her on the cheek again during the last trick. Janette slammed the boot and went back into the club, pushing her way through the double doors, she glanced at herself in the mirror. Her fake tan had begun to rinse off in the downpour, she looked like a clown who'd had a fight with a can of orange paint. She felt in her pocket and took out a coin, which she covered with one hand and then revealed her empty palm in the mirror. She knew a trick or two.

'Janette, the lovely Janette!' slurred Jason as she took a stool next to him at the bar. 'What you having my love?'

'Just a tonic water, thanks, I am driving.'

'Make it a slim line,' said Jason and slapped her hard on the bum.

Janette coolly scraped back her wayward hair from her ear and produced a slice of lemon and plonked it in her glass.

'All packed up are we?'

'Of course.'

'Wonderful, I might just slip down a cheeky chaser then.'

'You were amazing,' said Billy appearing from the kitchen with a cheese and pickle bap. 'I thought you'd really gone, really disappeared.'

'If only,' said Janette as she took another mouthful of her slim-line tonic.

Trees

Diana Newson

Trees have thrown outward their spiralled limbs,
unravelling and tattering in a growth explosion.

We can follow the tracks of the burst,
if we slow our blood; in stasis; the shock frozen.

Feel the release of those braced coils;
flickering blushes of fingers and leaves.

Around us the buildings are plunging like rainfall.
Our hearts, the slow stretching hearts of the
        trees.

Journey to Soweto

Rose Saliba

History was being made and Terrie wanted to be there to see it for herself. She wanted to hear the great Mandela speak, see how tall he really was, be there and feel the energy she had heard about. She knew her husband, Jeremiah, would never approve so she had to find a way to get out of the complex, away from the mining village and into the city, before he noticed she was missing.

That very morning he had been over-familiar with one of her maids. He was at it again, she was sure of it. Anyone would think it was the 1890s, not the 1990s, the way he carried on. Sometimes she hated him so much she wanted to kill him. She knew any attempt would be futile. He was surrounded by so many body guards as if he knew how much he was hated by the workers. He ran the mine like a prison and treated the miners as criminals. Everyone was searched coming off shift, every day. He was a big man and the power as manager had gone to his head.

Terrie, by contrast was diminutive in stature. She had been a pretty young girl, and was married off to him at a very young age. Now, at 29 with only two children and at least three miscarriages, she felt drained and betrayed. She wanted a better life for her daughters and herself, but knew that was never going to happen unless she produced a son. She had taken a good many beatings from her big ugly husband over the years for not doing so.

Her latest hope and hero was Nelson Rolihlahla Mandela, who had just been released from jail after 27 long years and was going to give a speech at a celebration rally in Soweto in two days' time. His wife Minnie would make things good for women in the future – she had promised. Things were going to change and get better. Terrie needed to believe that.

Her daughters, Lilley-Mae and Becka, were staying with their grandmother in Johannesburg, out of harms way. They were due a visit, but he didn't like her going. He never approved of anything at all. What made him like that? She wondered. Was it her fault? Was she not a good enough wife? Her mother kept telling her to keep her head down and her mouth shut. She had a good life and even had maids. The truth was that she would rather do the work herself and have a good husband. One she could talk to – one who saw her and listened to her.

Terrie rang her mother from the hall phone. It took ages to get through. When she did it was to a neighbour who had to go and get her. Eventually, she heard her mother wheeze into the receiver demanding to know what was so urgent. Terrie pretended her mother was saying one of the children was sick, in case anyone was listening in. Then said she would come straight away, leaving her mother confused at the other end of the phone.

Terrie stood very still when she hung up, to see if she had been overheard. She didn't trust that maid. No one was around. She went upstairs and found her travel bag and started to pack some clothes for the journey and for the girls. She went down to the kitchen and asked the cook to pack her up a lunch. She left a note for her husband saying it was an emergency and she would see him when she got back. Then she ordered the car.

The driver, George, was wary of her husband and was sure to tell Jeremiah where he had dropped her. Then he would follow her and bring her back. She had to time it exactly so the train left before the driver got back. She told him the same story and how worried she was about her daughter. He made sympathetic noises but she could tell he didn't really care and was scared he'd get into trouble. She decided being assertive was the only way to get him to do it. She was, after all, the lady of the house, so he worked for her too.

The station was 10 miles away and it would take another 4 hours to get to the city. She felt the adrenaline pump in her veins and a surge of excitement as they left the compound and headed out into the dust. She was on her way and grateful to her mother for suggesting that she put money away safely for when she needed it. She hoped she had enough.

After buying her ticket, Terry had to run to the platform and just caught the train. It pulled out of the station with a lot of noise and was so crowded she had to sit on her small case in the corridor for most of the journey. She was very glad of the lunch Cook had packed for her and only ate it when she was certain Jeremiah couldn't catch up with her. Perhaps he would forget about her and take up with the maid. Maybe she could stay with mother and her girls. He would never agree to that, and would stop sending the money needed to feed them as a way of punishing her.

The reunion with her children was tearful and strained; it had been so long. But they soon warmed up to her when she produced the sticky sweeties – to the sounds of her mother's protests. When they were asleep, Terrie explained to her that she was going to the rally and, after a great deal of argument, agreed to dress as a boy with some of the neighbours on a special bus out to Soweto's Soccer Stadium.

The next morning, Terrie joined the group on the church bus and waved to her mother and children who would all have loved to come too. When they arrived at the stadium, there were queues and queues of buses and people coming from everywhere. She learned later that there had been 120,000 people in the stadium – it certainly looked like the whole nation had turned up. The noise and the colours and the lightening bolts of energy and hope were going to be imprinted on her mind for ever. Life would never be the same again. He was here, Mandela, a dot in the distance and she was here, a speck in the crowd – making history...

Door

Paul Walker

My steps shorten as I approach the revolving door. It's turning slowly, but I can see the shape of a man in a flapping, light raincoat about to exit. I have to time this right or I will be caught by his push. Should I go now or hold back? I stretch my right leg, lunge and squeeze the cheeks of my buttocks together as I enter the space and shuffle out the other side into a grand, marbled atrium. I managed that without mishap, and perhaps it was a good omen for the ordeal ahead.

Third floor, second door on the right. I knock and wait for a muffled noise before entering. It's an ante room with two women and a man clacking away on computer keyboards. The woman closest to me acknowledges my name with the briefest of nods and points to a row of chairs outside a door. I sit down in the middle of the row feeling like a naughty schoolboy waiting to be chastised by the headmaster for peeking through a window into the girls' showers.

After a few minutes the same woman says, 'Sir Anthony will see you now,' and lifts a finger as if she resents the extra effort my presence has brought to her work. The office is imposing. Oil paintings of the worthy and famous decorate oak-panelled walls; a meeting table at one end is balanced by an enormous desk at the other; and a painting of the Queen and Sir Anthony crown the man himself seated in a studded, leather chair. He is writing on a piece of paper which is cast like a desert island in an ocean of highly-polished wood. I approach the chair opposite waiting for the command to be seated.

He looks at me and says, 'Sexual harassment.' His Scottish accent presents it more as an invitation to participate in a board game than an accusation. Before I have chance to gather my thoughts and respond he adds, 'Or, sexual abuse.' He unearths a folder from beneath the paper and continues, 'I have the whole sorry, story in this report from Pam in HR. Last day of the Brighton conference; you lure the complainant to your bedroom; force her to undress; she becomes fearful of your aggressive demeanour; somehow manages makes her escape before...' He runs his tongue around his mouth as if to remove an unpleasant taste and leaves the rest unsaid. 'To top it all, you threaten her with dismissal if she fails to comply with your grubby requests.'

'Almost all of that is untrue and...'

'Almost?' he interrupts and leans back in his chair.

'Well, she was in my room, but I didn't invite her. She was in my bed, naked, when I arrived there.' I hesitate as he swivels his chair and picks up a vibrating mobile phone. He presses twice with his index finger, replaces it and gestures for me to continue. 'I didn't lure her; she was pissed; I was sober; I refused to play her game and asked her to leave. I can only assume that she was offended by my rebuff and decided to take her revenge.'

I'm still standing and realise that I've been waving my hands, so place my legs apart and clasp my hands behind my back. I've left school and it seems that I'm now in the parade ground having a dressing-down from the sergeant-major, expecting to be put on *jankers*.

He rotates his chair from side to side for a few moments, then stops abruptly and places both his hands flat upon his desk. 'I'm disappointed, James. This doesn't look good; a senior member of my team accused of juvenile and threatening behaviour to one of his staff.' He drums his fingers on his desk and I adjust my feet waiting for the axe to fall. 'I can't have it... not here... looks bad... can't have...' His voice trails away and he clicks his tongue. His speech has a musical quality and his last statement reminds me of a chorus in a pop song; Lady Gaga, maybe?

The silence between us has been too long and I say, 'I'm innocent, it wasn't like that... really.' It sounds lame and unconvincing.

'You've got to go, James... but...' I wish he'd just get on with it and cease the dramatic pauses. '...you're one of my most promising young Turks and I'm loth to...'

What's this – a reprieve; a last-minute phone call from the palace?

'I'm moving you to New York. There's a vacant position out there that may suit. Go back to your office, clear your desk and wait for further instructions from HR. I'll want you to start there next week.'

I leave the office in a daze and wander down the edge of the wide, carpeted staircase until I reach the bottom. The revolving door in front of me is spinning as a cluster of dark-suited men enter and gaze at the splendour before them. I walk purposefully and confidently towards an inviting gap and emerge on the other side without breaking stride.

I think I handled that rather well.

Food

Diana Newson

"They're everywhere, the smooth little things. Look."

V lazily pushed the lens over to me and I peered through the translucency and down the optic pipe right out into mid-air.

"It makes me hungry just to see them," I said, appreciatively flexing my claws.

"It's worked beyond our wildest dreams," he said. "Well worth the wait." His eyelid throbbed gently in its calyx, a sign of satisfaction. I rustled closer and he quickly and deferentially moved away slightly.

"No one else must know. We must collect all the derivatives for our two Houses alone," I said.

"Shall we take one now? It's been a long trip...and I know you hate the dri-flake."

"Be careful, discriminate. A male only." I sent a little needle of cold into his brain. He didn't respond, instead almost seemed to enjoy it.

"I'll set up the farm," he said. "They need to be properly looked after."

* * *

She came round to her own incoherent whimpers of fear. It was dim, confusing, it stank and there was stinking muck in her hair. She could hear people around her, their voices bleating and yelping, hardly any words. The floor was rough, cold, and wet. She put a hand to her face, to push the hair out of her eyes, but couldn't feel her fingers and in the dim, mean light she stared in horror. *Her thumbs were gone.* The skin was hastily folded and coarsely stapled.

A near-by voice moaned "My hands, my hands."

They'd cut off peoples' thumbs. She lay completely still, her eyes widening to catch the tiniest spark of light and felt someone move next to her. She pressed into this human form like a child clinging to its parent, and he responded by pressing back. She realised they were naked but crushed closer.

"Have they cut off your thumbs?" her voice was an unbelieving whisper.

"My whole hands. My hands..." his voice was weak and she realised that they'd been treated in different ways, he had been hacked at, whereas her pain was distant and her wounds were closed.

"How...?"

"That machine with the blue wire," he groaned.

"I can't remember it," she said. "I must've passed out."

"Different...for men and women." He could hardly bear to speak with the pain and every breath was a sobbing groan.

"We must stand up," she said, and like desperate prey they hauled themselves to their feet, and stood swaying, arms encircling each other and staring blindly into the blackness. She could feel the blood running down her back from his wrists.

Above them a sudden circle of light blinked into existence. There was a great chattering of horror and a scramble to the edges of the pit away from the light. She dimly saw a nightmarish shape and then a tumble of children were thrown down among them. Some were screaming, some were numb with agony and terror.

"The boys..." she said, seeing them lying on the floor whimpering, with blood running from between their legs.

Death will be a relief, she thought, as she watched a brave thumbless woman try and comfort the children. The light above them vanished.

A slit opened in one side of the pit, and from the opposite side wriggled a thin streak of fire. It cracked against someone and they cried out struggling away from it. A smell of burning skin filled the pit and whimpering, they all crowded towards the opening. They crawled through it one-by-one, and up a slippery blue plastic ramp.

At the top were three ghastly doors, like open mouths, already dripping in blood from the ends of severed limbs. Men women and children. He was forced one way, she the other. There was incoherent screaming inside and outside her head.

* * *

"What did you get in the first scoop?" I asked.

"Males, females, and young," he answered. "They're coming up now."

"Males to the cull, females to the herd," I said. "How soon can we start impregnating females?"

"Straightaway," he said, and slyly looked at me out of one yellow eye. I let him have a little reward for his efficiency, delivered straight into the top of his ganglion.

"We've got some luscious young males. They've been de-handed and castrated and would make a nice gift."

"For my Queen?" I said.

"There's enough for both our Queens."

"Pen them under the white nets," I said. "We must stop them moving as soon as we can...for tenderness."

He bowed. Maybe he could have a physical gift tonight; he'd done well.

"Skins," I said.

"We're peeling some now, the skins will be ready soon."

"Have you called the render ships?"

"Of course."

"The real money will be in the unborn-torn." Longing and appetite entered my voice.

He nodded and said, "We could get one from the wild if you want one now; we'll have to wait for farmed."

The biology of the food dictated this, and however efficient he was he couldn't hurry it. He cringed slightly, expecting a punishment. I allowed my tongue to flicker over my teeth to put him at ease.

"Oh...but farmed is so much easier. We'll wait. It's not so long," I said, and V's melanophores flushed dark brown with pride and gratitude.

I leaned over the struggling flesh below.

"Look at that one," I said.

V came as close as he dared and followed my gaze.

"I wonder where he thinks he's going?" he said.

We watched in amusement for a bit longer.

"We will need to keep a male," I said, feeling a prick of interest in the one that didn't seem afraid to leave the herd.

"A biddable male, not him," said V firmly. I would have squirmed in pleasure at his tone if I hadn't been the Commander.

"You're the farmer," I said and watched as V changed the gradient and the male slid back among the others. They were on the moving belt now, towards the cutting floor.

It was comical to see them all struggling to go back the way they came, against the relentless belt and the outpouring from the pit. I watched my male looking wildly about, I could almost swear he caught my eye, although there was no meaning in his look. I was almost sorry when the hooks fell and swept him to dangle upside down in front of the rotating blade.

Boy in a Suitcase

Virginie Busette

This is the tale of the little boy that lived in a suitcase.
Not as strange as you may think actually, although if you are not Tom - explorer of worlds old and new - then you will think him to be at odds with the typical boys from his school.

Tom did not just live in his suitcase, he took it everywhere with him. As he says, "I like to just up and go at the last minute if needs be." In his opinion, his suitcase was the safest and fastest way to travel.

At six years old, Tom travelled to more places than all the pupils in his class, even more places than Arthur the school bully, who mocked him every time he came back from his world tours with new trinkets to show to his classmates.

Arthur would just yell at him, "I bet you got your mum to buy it from ebay on the Internet." One time even Mrs Pompew, Tom's teacher who had a passion for archaeology, could have sworn that the Egyptian amulet she was holding was the real deal, but how could this be possible?

What Mrs Pompew did not know, was that Tom had unlocked the magic to his travelling suitcase and of course, no grown up could know about it - only children could. However, even if Arthur opened and closed the suitcase a hundred times or tried to lock himself in, which he had done many times to try and visit the Blue Mountains in Australia, unless Tom shared the secret to the magic with another deserving child, suitcase travel would be impossible.

From an outsider's eye, suitcase travelling could seem a crazy idea and a little uncomfortable, but Tom could travel better than 1st class to all his destinations. No need to pack clothes, as some new ones were always available in the countries he visited when he checked in to the Suitcase Travel Club. Pretty handy when you time travel, actually!

No need to bring food. Tom preferred local food anyway, and how many times a week can you have spagboll really?

And he could eat as many sweeties and biscuits as he liked during the journey and drink litres of his favourite strawberry flavoured Long Island Smoothie.

But what Tom enjoyed the most was the entire week he could spend away in the space of one night because of magical time zones. There was always time for visiting monuments, shopping and meeting dignitaries during each trip and he was always back in time for school the next day. You see, jet lag is no issue with suitcase travel. A win-win situation really!

A Lucky Break

Sheila Molloy

They stuck me in Cafe Sausalito in The Fall, two months before The Big Day, so I'd look part of the furniture by then.

'Bilingual, are you?' Big Suit had asked.

'Yeah, mum was born in Madrid.'

'How come you're so lily white then, girl?'

'Daddy's Norwegian. Guess I inherited his genes.'

'OK. Here's the deal. Café's a big Hispanic hangout. You'll be our eyes and ears. Most important thing – don't react to anything said in Spanish. They can't know you "spika da lingo".' He laughed at what passed for wit in his world.

'They'll be more loose-lipped that way,' he continued. 'Reckon you can cope with that, girl?'

'Sure.'

'We can't tool you up. Not fitting for a waitress. Any trouble, Lofty in the kitchen's one of ours. He'll have your back.'

I nodded.

You could smoke in bars back then and it was like the whole town came into Café Sausalito to light up. It stank, and a grey stratus cloud was a permanent fixture below the yellowed ceiling. During my first week the clientele declared open season on my boobs and butt. You could grab women then without getting into trouble. As they fantasised in Spanish about what they wanted to do to me, I'd just act dumb. Flash them a smile. Men had been talking dirty to me long as I could remember. No big deal.

A group of four were of particular interest. They always sat in the corner table at the back where the light was dim and the smoke thickest. Mostly they spoke in whispers so it was difficult to eavesdrop, but I'd picked up enough to know they were no patriots. Big Suit told me to keep listening.

The fella who did most talking had ebony, slicked-back hair, a boozer's bulbous nose and a pouchy face pockmarked with bristles. He always seemed on edge. Couldn't keep still. He'd slice the air with his hand. Slap the table with a big, meaty fist. Wag his fat index finger at the others 'til they dropped their eyes. If he wanted serving, he'd grunt a command. Once he slapped my butt so hard he left a bruise. He laughed when he saw brief anger flare in my eyes, showing the inside of a mouth filled with uneven, gold-capped teeth.

On The Big Day, the four were sitting in their usual place and I was wiping down the next table's red Formica top with my back to them. That's when I heard something that stilled the breath in my throat. For just a second, I stopped. I clenched the cloth in my fist, then willed my arm to keep on cleaning.

When I turned round, I couldn't help flicking him a quick glance. He was staring at me with hard, dark eyes, rubbing his top lip, his other hand rolled round the arm of the chair like a big cat ready to pounce.

Our eye contact was brief. But that's all it took. He knew I'd understood every word. Painting a smile on my face, I sauntered towards the kitchen door aware of the sibilance of whispering reaching a crescendo behind me. I heard a chair scrape across the wooden floor. When I saw Lofty wasn't in the kitchen I fled out back into the alley. Sprinted between the trash. Snatching a look behind, I saw him running. He moved quick for a big man.

The sidewalks were jammed because of The Big Day. Some streets cordoned off. Families, kids, oldies - all there, excited and waving their flags, making a collective happy buzz like bees in a hive. I was on fast forward. They were idling, so it was hard pushing through them, spoiling their mood. I darted into an open door in a big warehouse on Elm and ran up the stairs to the first floor, then just carried on up, passing landing after landing, all of them smelling of old paper. Muscles screaming, I stopped to get my, breath, holding my knees and filling my lungs. A breeze from behind floated across my back swiftly cooling the sweat. Turning, I saw it came from a large, open window, where clouds leisurely scudded past. Hands on the sill I leaned out and saw the crowds below with their flags, kids on shoulders, police keeping them back from the street. I'd got a great view of Main. Then I heard a faint creak on the stair and spun round, back to the window, hands clutching the sill each side of me.

His face showed no emotion as he raised the gun. I stood there. Waited for the end.

I should have died. Couldn't process what happened at the time but afterwards I realised there must have been a break in the clouds. A great slab of yellow-white light had flooded the landing and blinded him. The bullet whizzed past me through the window, adrenaline kicked in and I ran for my life.

Out in the street, pushing, shoving and getting away, the crowd sounded different. No longer the contented, happy buzz of anticipation. People were swarming aimlessly; screaming, crying, going too fast, bearing me along on a massive tide of panic and fear.

'Why are we going already?' cried a little boy perched on his daddy's shoulders. 'I don't understand. What's happened, Pa?'

'Someone shot the president, son.'

Lost and Found

Charlotte McDermott

'Don't cry Robbie, believe me, you've had it if they see you crying.'

I look up at my father twiddling his moustache nervously and I squeeze my eyes tight, in the hope that the tears will go back to where they came from. I feel wobbly and mixed up about everything. I keep thinking about my new train set and hoping Charlie won't ruin it while I am away. I think about Nancy and the teddy she gave me but my father told me to leave behind. I think about the fields behind my house and the den that we made yesterday.

My mother has a new hat; she looks beautiful. My father said it on the way here but she just looked out of the window and said nothing. She probably has one of her heads. She is squeezing her handkerchief and it is making her knuckles white. I think she must be angry with me but I don't know why.

* * *

'My name is Mrs Jesson and I am the Matron here at
Fortismere. Say goodbye to your parents, boys and line up for
your number.'

Mrs Jesson is tall and thin with a grey bun. She has a
pimply thing on the end of her nose that bobs up and down
when she speaks. My father straightens my cap, 'Well this is it
young man, time to go. We'll see you at Christmas, the weeks
will rush by.'

My mother bends down and kisses me on the cheek. She
smells of lavender.

'Be a good boy Robbie.'

I walk into the line with the other boys and we watch our
parents leave, some of the mothers are crying and waving
frantically. I watch the backs of my parents and see my father
ty to take my mother's hand, but she moves it away quickly. I
am given a number, 132, but I have no idea why. When they
call 132 I don't step forward because I don't understand what
they want me to do.

'It's your peg and your bed.' Says a little boy with a snotty
nose.

I notice that he has wiped it on the back of his hand and
has a dried crusty layer of snot there.

'You're next to me, I am 133.'

I nod in agreement but I still don't really know what he
is talking about. The matron tells us to follow one of the big
boys who says his name is Wilson and we are in his House.
Does that mean we will be living in his house? I am really not

sure but I follow him and the snotty kid as we walk up the enormous staircase. We enter a room that has rows of beds and numbers just above them. There are older boys sprawled on their beds who jump up and look busy when Wilson walks in. These are the dorms that my father said would be jolly good fun, but I can't see how, when all there are beds.

Wilson tells us to wash our hands and get ready for dinner. I feel my tummy and realise that I am quite hungry.

'Make sure you use soap, Andrews.' Wilson is talking to me but he doesn't call me Robbie, he is using my second name.

I realise that Wilson probably isn't his first name either. As I try to dry my hands, one of the older boys with ginger curly hair shoves my shoulder. He doesn't say sorry. The snotty kid tugs my arm and I follow him to the dining hall. Matron comes to check we are eating all our food. She stands and watches as I wrestle the pieces of pie into my mouth. It tastes horrible, but I am too afraid not to eat it all up like a good boy.

When I go back to the dorm there is no sign of my pyjamas that were folded and put on my pillow. I look around, but all the boys are the same and I don't take someone else's. You'd better look in 'Lost and Found' says the snotty kid, but I have no idea what he is talking about. My bed looks strange; it is a darker colour in the middle. I touch it and it is wet. I haven't spilt anything on it. How can it have got wet?

'That used to happen to me,' says the snotty kid, wiping his nose on the back of his hand.

Switch

Virginie Busette

The boys were silent in their contemplative appreciation. A real live bomb. In their garden. Well...it looked real.

Korr quickly caught Zephs's arm interrupting its ascension towards the red glowing light at its centre.

"Are you insane Zephs?' You should know better than to touch a throbbing, glowing device which is clearly not from this world. Have you not learned anything from your classes?"

"This is a 30th century Earth relic by the looks of it, and don't question my knowledge please, you know I'd beat you at any Earth Primitive History tests."

Happy with his retort, Zephs withdrew his arm and looked at his brother asking more to himself than to Korr.

"The real question is how did it get here – and a live one at that?"

They knew that the presence of this live weapon was impossible. The campaign to annex all planets in the Earth's galaxy had taken care of that long ago. Earth had disappeared when it was time for the universe realignment to be finalised.

A mistake, according to Korr. Avid student of History of The Covenant Wars, he could see that the decision was short-sighted, but the leaders of the Council had considered that Earth rendered a dead planet was wasted space and did not qualify for terraforming.

Earth people had expanded their knowledge of the universe and were known to be undisputed experts in the space mapping and time travel fields. For that knowledge, they had been spared but scattered to all corners of the universe for fear that one day they would rise against the Council. Their sentence had been harsh. Some thought it had been "tampered with" to benefit the Lunar colony.

As they had watched the blue and green of their planet disappear into nothingness, Lothar, leader and wisest amongst all Earth men, spoke his last words before a guard's spear sent him to his death, but not before he promised revenge on the Council.

He spoke, "Through space and time, you will run. Our fury will be your end."

These centuries-old words are still present in today's younglings' history books.

Zephs snapped back to reality showing a fear in his eyes that froze Korr on the spot; a sight he'd never expected to see in his brother. And when the "click" resounded in the air silencing every other sound around them, they knew for certain that Earth people had returned.

"Zephs...run!" were the only words Korr had time for before the bomb went off.

A coughing fit dragged Korr back into consciousness. His eyes stung, he was sure they were opened, but he could only see darkness. His head was throbbing and the sound of a heavy chain cut short the involuntary move of his right leg. As he made sense of his surroundings, he quickly became aware of the walls of his cell. Although he did not know who had made him prisoner, he was certain that the blast should have killed them both.

"Zephs! Where is Zephs?" he shouted in the dark. "Where is my brother? Whoever you are, you will never get away with this. Do you hear me?"

With those last words suspended in the air, Korr let out a harrowing scream. The anger and the pain contained within it, were unmistakable, but so was the sound of the key unlocking his cell.

"Korr, first son of Kesh, you will stand, or I will make you."

As his vision captured the light entering his cell, Korr reluctantly stood up. The approaching shadow took the shape of a familiar man that he could not quite place. And then it hit him.

"You are Lothar. But how? You should have died long ago."

"I did," said Lothar as he approached Korr. "Guilty of no crime, but executed without trial at the hands of your people."

Looking straight into Lothar's eyes, it was as if Korr could reach in the past and see it all. The day that should never have been: Lothar's last words before the spear took him. Breaking eye contact with his jailor, Korr asked again about his brother and why they had been brought here.

"You are braver than most, standing up to your captor, I'll give you that. But it's our knowledge and not our home that The Council should have taken."

"Earth will be made whole again, Son of Kesh."

As he walked away to exit the cell, Lothar looked at Korr once more and said, "There is more than one way to realign a universe."

The light in the cell left with Lothar and the sound of the locking key followed. Alone in the dark again, a sense of dread filled Korr.

Lucky Lucy Valentine

Imelda Harrison

L ucky Lucy Valentine - yes, that was her name, because she met her lucky Larry, the man in her life, on the 14th Feb 1994. Larry was the one alright.

They got married that very day and went away on the 16th February, it was love at first sight. They flew to Jersey in the Channel Isles for their honeymoon. They had a really great time and returned, to start their married life in a two up, two down semi-detached house in Baldock.

Well, the problem wasn't with Larry; it was with Lucy. Larry – plumber by trade - went away to work each day and arrived home after a hard day's graft, hungry and tired. As soon as he opened the front door and stepped inside the hallway, he immediately thought the house was on fire. There was the most terrible, stifling stench coming from the kitchen. There was smoke creeping out from under the kitchen door. The dinner was burnt.

"Oh no, oh lor!" he cried and gasped for breath. But he was calm and the most patient, most tolerant man she could have wished for.

"Lucy," he called, "Are you alright? Will you please come downstairs? We've had a fire."

"I know," she said, looking down at him in a carefree way, "I was just having a read in my bedroom."

"You've burnt our meal again."

Lucy stood there staring into space, mouth agog, as though she had not even remembered cooking it. "But we've got no dinner now," she said going a very peculiar colour.

"That's right," Larry replied looking at her quizzically with compassion and slight frustration. "I'll tell you what," he suggested putting his arm around her, 'I'll get a take-away."

Lucy looked into his eyes and thanked him. "I love you," she said, smiling, "And I'll make you breakfast in the morning."

Half an hour later, Larry arrived back with a takeaway Chinese chicken chow mein, which they enjoyed with a glass of wine.

This peculiar behaviour went on for two years. Burnt breakfasts, burnt dinners and so on. Larry was losing weight and getting thinner. He'd hardly eaten anything she'd cooked and yet he never grumbled or bore malice at anything that Lucy did wrong, He put up with a lot because he loved her. Lucy was lucky. She'd really got away with murder. Larry was still happy. He had the most attractive smile. Had it been infatuation with Lucy? Nobody really knew the reason for her strange behaviour. And so it continued.

Then, one night a strange thing happened. Larry had arrived home from a party for his mother's birthday. He was still smiling. Lucy did not go with him that particular night. As he walked in through the door he could smell smoke. He was suddenly cautious, thinking he could smell gas. He grabbed his torch, there was a smell of gas from the unlit fire. Larry quickly turned it off and opened the windows. He found Lucy in the chair. She was asleep. There was something weird. It wasn't any normal sleep. Lucy was not responding at all. She was unconscious.

Larry couldn't believe this was happening. He phoned for an ambulance. Perhaps, he thought, there might be some chance of the paramedics reviving her. He wept bitterly beside the chair while he was waiting. His dear wife Lucy. She couldn't cook for toffee, but he still loved her and in a strange way, she had loved him too, or did she? They had been a valentine couple.

Later, the ambulance arrived and in time she recovered. Had she tried to end it all? She hadn't realised she'd done it. Larry forgave her. He was that glad she survived her apparent suicide. It was such a shock for poor Larry. All he could say at that moment was, "Lucy please don't ever try to do that again. I love you." He kissed her. She was amazed at his reaction, apologised and promised to attend cookery classes.

Printed in Poland
by Amazon Fulfillment
Poland Sp. z o.o., Wrocław